The High-Pitched Laugh of a Painted Lady

The High-Pitched Laugh of a Painted Lady

Stories by Lewis W. Green

JOHN F. BLAIR, Publisher
Winston-Salem, North Carolina

Library of Congress Cataloging in Publication Data

Green, Lewis W   1932–
    The high-pitched laugh of a painted lady.

        CONTENTS: Chaingang preacher.—The high-pitched laugh
of a painted lady.—The burial of Big Blue. [etc.]
        I. Title.
PZ4.G796Hi   [PS3557.R373]   813'.54   80–16382
ISBN 0–89587–017–7
ISBN 0–89587–020–7(pbk.)

To
BRENNAN,
PATRICK,
and
EGAN

Contents

Contents

The
High-Pitched
Laugh
of a
Painted
Lady

Chaingang Preacher

THE PEACHTREE PRISON CAMP WAS AN ISO-
lated stronghold in Cherokee County, which was the
mountainous westernmost county of the state. Two other
states' lines were nearby, and this fact kept alive a certain
possibility among the convicts. If one escaped across a state
line, there was a great advantage. Even if one was caught,
extradition was a tedious affair, and there would be some time
to rest in jail before being returned to the road camp.

These circumstances did not add considerably to Captain
Aud's sense of despair; he was a stoic and endured his job as
road-camp superintendent. Yet he was not bitter. His years of
service to the Democratic Party had been rewarded by the
superintendency. It was a good job, and steady jobs were scarce
in the mountains. Nothing else had as much security except
jobs in the school system, and he had neither the education nor
the pull to get anything better than a school bus driver's job.

Captain Aud knew that he would not rise higher, that he
could not have accommodated the pressures of a bigger job
anyway. Yet he also knew that he would not lose his job unless
there was a spectacular riot or mass escape. All he had to do
was to keep things quiet and manageable. He had learned that
long-time convicts or lifers were not to be unduly harassed
about minor matters. So he extended a reasonable indulgence,
a subtle system of minute privilege which did not interfere
with discipline or compromise himself and his guards in the
state's view. Aud's guards and gun-captains—to the man gaunt,
quiet mountaineers, quick of mind, easy in movement—were so

instructed. They all knew that the camp's life was divided into zones of influence and hidden administration and that the convicts had control over the major share. Only with their silent acquiescence did things go smoothly on any given day. To the guards, that did not matter. In watching over the convicts they acquired a convict set of mind; they too watched over the flow of time, building their hours, watching the days slip away.

The prison grapevine is generally a trustworthy medium which moves information at varying speed and detail. If the first flash is somewhat in error, built-in mechanisms eventually adjust to accuracy. Time is not of the essence in the grapevine carrying raw intelligence which must be sifted through. Still the convicts often knew of events that would affect them before the superintendent knew.

So by the grapevine, they learned that one Balky Guffin was coming to Peachtree. They knew he was coming even before he was tried and sentenced, and they knew it this way:

Peachtree needed a trusty, a misdemeanant, to serve as a waterboy and tool-grinder for the Gunter crew of hard-rock felons in the road gang. Their last trusty, Charlie Sorrells, had run off not once, but three times, automatically qualifying himself to be a felon and join the same road gang he had once served as trusty. While waiting for sentencing in the Waynesville jail, Sorrells had met Balky Guffin, who was awaiting trial on the various misdemeanors of making moonshine liquor, hauling it, resisting arrest, assaulting an officer, and other related, smaller charges which would become negotiable between defense and prosecution when trial time came. The charges were deliberately so consolidated as to cause the bail to be too high for Balky to make. Conviction was foreordained—the powers who settle these things had decided that Balky was due for a lesson.

Since Balky Guffin was a first offender, a war veteran, and a native mountaineer and had part of a college education, Sorrells divined that he was a likely candidate to be sent to Peachtree as trusty. When "Runnin' Charlie" returned to the chaingang, he told them about Balky.

Peachtree Camp's pickup truck pulled into the parking lot in front of the prison office. The caged truck bed was full of new convicts from the Haywood term of court, and with a few transfers from the Whittier camp. It was midafternoon and most of the camp's population was out working the right-of-way along the highways. But three or four guards in the small office building filed out with shotguns and 30-30s and directed the convicts inside. A guard called for Balky Guffin.

"Yes. Here," the young man said. Pale from the Haywood jail, he was nondescript and undistinguishable except for feverish black eyes, which were at once worried, smiling, and guarded.

"You Guffin?" the guard asked gruffly.

"Yeh. I wouldn't have said it if I wasn't."

"Well, you're supposed to be trusty, but I'm damned if I know how long that'll last if you keep talking back like 'at 'air. You come on with me down to the cellblocks."

The guard left his shotgun in the guardroom adjoining the office and walked behind Balky to the wire gate and unlocked it. Then he took him to a squat, square building where they waited for a guard inside to unlock the door.

"He's gon' be trusty fer the Gunter squad. Let him go ahead and fix up a bunk in that squad. When he gets done, bring him back up to the office and get his pitcher took and his prints rubbed," the guard said.

The new guard looked at Balky, then smiled weakly.

"Well," he said. "You ain't sich a big feller to cause all that trouble and fight the law like you did. We was 'spectin' a bad ass when we heard you was comin'."

Balky gave him a quick, bright grin, but smothered it immediately. No threat emanated from the second guard, who took him to the supply shed to get a suit of blue denim clothes, shoes and socks, two sheets, a pillow and pillowcase, and two

Army blankets. They returned to the cellblock, and Balky was let into his section. The guard said, "Let me know when you're done. You have to go back up to the office," and walked away.

Balky had already noticed in the hallway beyond the barred door a small clutter of cartons, which had once contained the candy, cookies, and tobacco products stacked on the shelves of the prison canteen, just above a locked soft-drink box. Inside, the cellblock was a wide, long dormitory, and Balky found an empty bunk for himself about halfway from where a pot-bellied stove in the center of the barracks smoldered with the remains of a fire. He made his bed and rested a moment at the foot of his bed on a wooden box, which would be his locker.

Only then did he allow himself to consider the thing that was totally out of keeping in the dull, spartan barracks. A construction of hanging cloth—a veritable Arabian tent—hung from a top bunk and completely covered the lower bunk.

"By God, the camp psycho lives here," Balky breathed in awe. He walked over to inspect the collection of materials— some rayon, some silk, but the large side slopes were of mattress ticking. Secured by ropes at the top and at the sides, the tent enclosed the floor space between two bunks. Guffin looked around to be certain that he was still alone in the cellblock, then he parted the draperies. Inside was a low wooden box— one of the crude lockers, except that this one was set up as an altar. On it was a leather etching, a portrait in crude bas-relief, a rough image of the crucified Christ. Never had Balky imagined such agony on Christ's face as he saw before him. He was immediately depressed; indeed, he felt as if he had stumbled on a corpse laid out in the wrong room. He wondered why, if Jesus had endured such pain as to leave that tortured expression on his face, he had not recanted and gone back to carpentry. Mankind seemed unworthy of all that pain. Hurriedly Balky pulled his head out of the tent and readjusted the draperies, but he was still depressed when the guard came to take him to the office.

Most of the other convicts had been processed and were lounging on the grass between the office and the fence. Balky had finished with his photos and fingerprints when the squad trucks began rolling in about two hundred feet away and unloading the road crews. Guards searched them before they straggled quietly to their barracks.

But one low cry from the convicts carried to the new men. "Fresh meat!"

A small man flushed and stirred nervously on the grass. Balky grinned.

"Listen, man," he said, "I built time in the Camp Lejeune Brig. There was some of that, but nobody does anything you don't let 'em do."

"I don't give a shit. By God, they better not . . ."

He looked at Balky's youthful face, was suddenly puzzled, and said, "Why you yourself . . ."

"No," said Balky. "That ain't what I'm worrying about."

Then the new convicts were taken to their cellblocks and turned in with the general population. Balky went to his locker and sat down, waiting for questions about the outside world. Strangely, no one approached him. The cons stayed around their own bunks. There was some quiet, desultory small talk. There were all kinds of men—strong, weak, and those whose faces and carriage showed that they had lived in poverty and defeat on the outside. There were demented men, haunted—watchers, all of them.

Watchers of Balky, of each other, of the windows and the far frosty mountains held in the last grip of winter, they were watchers of time, of smothering days piling upon them as they strained at their long, hopeless sentences, ranging up to double life imprisonment. They left him to himself. At first he caught a few glances of studied vacancy—at his unshackled ankles—then they did not look at him at all. Yet he knew he was being thoroughly examined and studied. Never had he felt such an urgent need for a friend. Yet he sat quietly, trying to show courtesy, for he sensed a deep tide of blood and dark, angry murder running where one might feel it but never quite see it until the fury was unleashed.

Balky cut his eyes about, panic rising almost uncontrollably. He could not avoid staring at their ankles, where each man had thick bands of steel, and hooked securely to each shackle was a two-foot length of logging chain. Their steps were measured, and there was a soft clink as they moved their feet from time to time.

Balky looked at the tent, but no one seemed to belong there. Then a guard unlocked the cellblock door and let two more men inside. There was no mistaking one of them. The flaring red beard and deep, wild eyes marked his messianic fervor. The preacher strode by Balky with a ponderous, rattling step. Like the others, he seemed unaware of the new man. He was followed by a twisted, bent little man. Dragging their chains, they made for the cloth tent. It was obvious that the smaller man was at the service of the preacher. When they reached the bunks, the preacher said, "Up, Woodrow!" as though to a dog, and the dwarf leaped to the top bunk and lay silent, panting slightly.

Balky felt a slither of fear when the preacher passed by. He had felt the intensity of the man, the threat and danger radiating from him. A glimmer of caution had come to the eyes of the others. Balky figured that the preacher exerted no small influence in here, and his own ingrained skepticism did nothing to dispel his fright. He sat blankly while the moments passed. Then a bell rang outside, and they lined up and were taken down the back steps, into the mess hall. There was no pushing or crowding. Each man fell into line where his place had been determined a long time ago. The strongest ones were in front. As a matter of prudence, Balky went to the end of the line. He added another observation to his store—the preacher and Woodrow were nowhere near the head of the line. So, he mused, there are some here who have settled scores with the preacher in the past. But a small band of apparently weak-witted creatures stood with the preacher.

In the mess hall, Balky's eyes again found the red-beard. How could one's eyes have missed him? Some of his weak followers clustered about him at the table in a distortion of a Biblical feast. They ingratiated themselves with the preacher at every chance. Happily they pressed on him all he wanted of the condiments they had received from home—mustard, horseradish, ketchup, onions, vinegar, hot peppers—those many things used to camouflage the drab taste of beans and potatoes and fatback.

In sullen order the prisoners finished eating, emptied and stacked the trays, then clanked their way back to the cellblocks for the final shakedown of the night. Last were the preacher and his entourage, who stroked their chins wisely as the preacher counseled from works written and unwritten. Pompously, as though they were the temple's elect, they stepped high in their chains. Close behind the preacher crept Woodrow, keeping an ear cocked for any command from the master.

Soon, in the vicinity of the tent, began such a service as Balky Guffin had not dreamed of in his wildest deliriums—and once he had gone to a snake-handling service, drunk enough to take part. The convicts not involved with the preacher appeared not to notice. The preacher went to his locker and pulled out a Bible. Then a half-dozen convicts pulled their lockers together and sat down, their hands clasped before them. Their eyes immediately glazed over—as though they had long been conditioned—and small, animal noises escaped their lips, although the preacher had yet to open his mouth.

The preacher strode with quick, powerful steps to the stove, as if it were a pulpit, put down his thick Bible, and let it fall open. Then he began to preach. The congregation fell silent. The preacher did not speak very loud, as if his covenant with the other convicts included a codicil that his noise would not intrude too much upon their silent construction of time.

Balky sat on his bunk, also pretending not to notice but burning with both fear and interest. He had the feeling that sooner or later the preacher was going to start pushing him, and while he would fight for any man's right to believe as he would, Balky would not let himself be tyrannized with religion. Balky liked honest discussion and open debate. He had learned that at college.

The preacher's stream-of-consciousness sermon flowed on, wild and unedited, filled with error and misquotation—long emotional paragraphs of speech, broken only when he inhaled loudly, reedily.

". . . The Lord sent me in here specially fer you 'uns," he said again and again as his brain sought for something else to say. Finally, ". . . yas, the Lord sent me in here to take care of you 'uns that are lost. Have no doubts, chillun, but that's whut happen . . ."

His parishioners nodded solemnly. A cynical thought crossed Balky's mind. It was a judge who had sent the preacher here for a long time. How was he going to thank God for that? The preacher's voice suddenly rose until it jarred the windows, and the grim faces of the other convicts turned to him until he brought it down a little. Then the preacher leveled straight at Balky, who tried to ignore the pointed references: ". . . a new lamb among us who has not received nor taken unto him the sanc-ti-fied word, *gasp, gasp,* who remains lost and sinful in sin, *gasp, gasp,* oh Heavenly Father have mercy, *gasp, gasp,* who will not be washed through the blood of the innercent lamb, *gasp,* praise God amen oh brothers lead him gently through the darkness toward the kind light an' out of that hellish pit oh Lord praise thy holy name and grant good Father that the new man will see the error and mistake of his wanderin' trail that led him to us and join us here tonight on thy altar . . ."

Balky sat embarrassed, looking first at his stiff new prison shoes, then at the darkness outside. The tempo increased—a quiet hum underlay the throb of the preacher's voice—and the listeners grew so drunk on their moanings and implorings that they seemed to forget Balky and concentrate on their own fugue.

Presently they swayed and sang softly. Five of them carried an off-key desecration of "The Old Rugged Cross." The preacher shoved Woodrow inside the tent, and the singing rose higher. There! thought Balky. He's going to do it as sure as hell. The singing grew louder, but it didn't hide Woodrow's whimpers of pain. After a few moments, the preacher emerged, a wild-eyed spectre from hell. Seconds later, Woodrow emerged, but his glum face revealed nothing. His clothing was not disarranged, so Balky dismissed homosexuality.

Then the preacher took another of his lambs behind the cloth, while the others massacred "Shall We Gather at the River?" Loud moans issued forth, and the singing grew higher. The preacher came out of the tent, followed by the convert. This one was subdued and stunned, as though he had seen beyond the veils into truth. The preacher returned to his ranting after two severely garbled verses of "Rock of Ages." Then suddenly, to Balky's eternal gratitude, the night guard pounded on the bars with his club and shouted:

"Now hush up, Reverend. You're bothering the citizens and taxpayers down the road, and yer likely to wake up the dead in the Murphy graveyard."

"Indeed. Yes indeed," muttered Balky.

The little prayer meeting dissolved, and soon the lights in the cellblock went out, leaving only the ones in the hall outside to cast dim illumination into the cell. Balky occupied a few minutes unobtrusively watching the convicts get out of their clothing with the leg-irons on their ankles.

Then his days began building. Before they would allow him the tasks of a trusty, he had to work for six weeks as a member of the gun-squad. It was a tortuous, ankle-twisting job. The convicts had to climb along the steep banks beside the public highways and cut back the brush along the right-of-way. If one didn't cut the brush to the very level of the ground, either he or the one following him could get his chains tangled or caught and go sprawling. Those who had worked for a long time moved on the banks and through the ditches quite nimbly.

Early spring came, and faint life began to stir in the gray, quiet faces of the convicts as pretty girls in their convertibles passed along the road. That was every convict's favorite fantasy—a beautiful girl would stop and spirit him away in her long, sleek car. The work went on. The squad was strung out in a line along the roadsides with a shotgun-armed guard at each end so that no man made a move unobserved. To answer the call of nature, one must call "Gettin' out, Cap'n," and get permission; even then a guard watched closely to be sure it was a true call of nature and not the siren call of freedom, coming from the woods and the hills.

Yes, a convict gettin' out had better deposit something upon the ground or the guard might conclude that he had it in his mind to run. Ah, it was hard for Balky Guffin to accustom himself to answering a call with the stern gaze of the guards on his hindparts.

Later in the season, when the temperatures had risen and late spring came, the convicts spent as much time chopping up rattlesnakes and copperheads as they did cutting down bushes. If someone inadvertently slammed his bush-axe into a low hornets' nest, then the entire line of convicts had to freeze in dread and frustration while the angry insects swarmed out and stung where they would. No man could risk making a sudden move lest the guards misread his intentions and blast away with their shotguns.

Balky made honor grade. Out from under the gun.

At noon he broke out the thermal cans of tepid beans and boiled potatoes and an occasional ribbon of fatback. The cons sat down and wolfed the poor fare. After twenty minutes—the length of time for the meal and two cigarettes rolled from

Bull Durham—it was back to the steep road banks . . . chop, chop, whick, whack, chop, chop, chop . . .

The men were hardened. Lesser men could not have lifted their feet to drag the chains past midafternoon. Yet on they went, the uneven line, chopping with slow, deliberate, and effective swings. Simple. Like Zen.

Each afternoon Balky staggered wearily through the shake-down at the gate and to his bunk, where he collapsed until the supper bell. Then he tottered stiffly into the line, went to the mess hall, and chewed in exhaustion. He was too miserable to know or care what transpired around him. Blisters swelled out of his palms, toughened to callus. The joints of his knuckles swelled from the unrelenting lifting and chopping. But he hardened, grew stronger. He was dimly aware that almost nightly the preacher and his little band held services, but in his exhaustion he cared not at all. It was merely another part of his bad dream.

Finally he became conscious once again of the nuances of life around him, and pondered them. In the college dormitory where he had lived, a certain camaraderie had prevailed. The same spirit had existed in the Marine barracks, even in the post brig at Lejeune—where the labor was harder than at Peachtree. There the men had had conversations, animosities, friendships. And the feeling of companionship should have been here among these robust, toughened men after a day's hard toil. But it was not. Each man seemed to be sunken into himself— into a small cell inside the bigger cell. Balky noticed a silent, invisible tumult, a barely contained pressure that built from the reluctant regret of past crime, detection, and separation from the rest of humanity.

As soon as dinner was over, most of the men went to their leatherwork, and there they remained, bitter and private. Some made rings from spoons stolen from the mess hall; others made variegated rings from the celluloid and plastic of old toothbrushes. They sold their handiwork out on the road when the guards would allow them to approach unapprehensive passers-by. The convicts left their bunks only to clank their way to the pissery, or go to the barred door and buy a soft drink and a moon pie from the canteen in the hall. A quiet, wary world—many worlds, off to themselves, in each other's orbit, but not connecting at all. Yet the cellblock had structure, its own language, gestures, and signals, undecipherable to anyone except its inhabitants. Balky learned the language and the rules. For instance, if a con decided to break out, he went in the cellblock one afternoon and put his cap down behind the stove. Throughout the rest of the day, his cellmates would saunter by and, at some time before the lights went out, unobtrusively drop in whatever small amounts of money they could afford. If any item of civilian clothing had been smuggled in, it too was left. Under the stove was a set of files—each man understood that they were to be used only on the chains or shackles, and not the bars on the windows, which would result in their discovery by Aud or some of his men. If someone left his cap behind the stove, he must run within the week. There was no returning the money, and no keeping it. A man who asked in this way for help had better try to make the run—a moment of truth, a rite of passage it was. Otherwise, the knives in the cellblock would deal harshly with him.

Balky still felt the fine line of mutual fascination between himself and the preacher. He pondered on the curious mixture of illiteracy, ignorance, religiosity, craftiness, and misguided sincerity in the man; he kept his thoughts hidden. And the preacher, it seemed, could not get a clear perception of this Balky Guffin, who was clearly stamped with the features, gestures, and accent of a mountaineer—yet who seemed more clever, more traveled and worldly, and more likely to ridicule him, to disbelieve. The preacher feared some dread discovery.

Balky watched him secretly. A brawny barrel of a man with swollen biceps bulging under his shirtsleeves. The beard was coarse, but neat nonetheless, and was as red as his hair. Both hair and beard underwent a clumsy, but regular, trimming at the hands of little, humped Woodrow. The preacher's blunt nose moved constantly, the nostrils opening and shutting as if each hot thought from his mind tripped an electric eye as it breathed out. Power radiated from him, and at times his eyes glowed like volcanic craters shimmering with inner heat. Contrasting with all this physical vitality were his obscene hands—ghastly long claws, tapered, hands which could have been taken from the corpse of a large woman and grafted onto those powerful arms. His hands were only slightly tanned despite the outdoor work, and they were curiously smooth—incongruous and vulgar against the rough bulk of the man. And in all of his secret observations, Balky Guffin never recalled seeing the preacher, working or resting, without a film of sweat on his brow and upper lip. It was as though the furnace of his fevered intent refused to be banked down, even in the cool of the mountain evenings.

No matter where the preacher moved, he was trailed by the pale and ugly little man. It was obvious that Woodrow didn't follow the preacher because he wanted to, but because he was afraid not to. If he strayed too far, a wild light came into those deep caverns above the red shaggy beard, and the commanding call went out: "Woodrow! Woodrow!"

The days came and went—each a drop of water eroding the sentence of Balky Guffin. He became a full trusty with the run of the camp, entering and leaving the cellblock as he wished, traveling to the supply house, to the office outside the fence, even to the little store down the road and to the small huts where the bloodhounds were kept. On afternoons when he had to remain at camp, he was allowed to take a fishing pole and go alone through the woods to the river. But most of his days were spent as waterboy for the gun-squad. The guards rode in a small, drab trailer behind the convict truck to keep the convicts from jumping off the truck bed and running, and sometimes Balky rode with them. The trailer was shaped like a wide, glass-fronted coffin bent at a 45-degree angle and mounted on an axle. Underneath the guards' seat were stored the axes, shovels, picks, bush-axes, sledgehammers, and go-devils, and the grindstone. Each morning when the truck arrived at the place where the squad would begin work, it was Balky's task to take out the grindstone, mount it on the truck's tailgate, and sharpen the convicts' tools, as needed. Sometimes to kill time, the convicts would choose a smooth rock—kept for years—and after their blade had been ground on the grindstone, they would hone it sharper by hand with their "whit-rocks."

Balky ground axes and watched. If a worker wanted water, he yelled, "Waterboy!" Balky would tote the zinc bucket and dipper to him. An efficiency expert would notice that the squad—in all its endeavors, in its every movement—slopped and spilled a few seconds here, a couple of minutes there. If the mood was on the squad, the work went smoother than any machine could have done it; but if it was not ready to work, there were frequent calls for water. It was "Gettin' out, Cap'n" here and it was a sprained ankle or a cut foot over there. The guards patrolled the line of work, uneasy, trying to catch the mood and ride it out, unless the malingering got too severe.

Balky watched Woodrow with utter fascination. The others moved awkwardly in their chains along a bank, chopping in a relatively straight line, leveling a patch of brush, then leap-frogging it to another clump. Not Woodrow. He hopped up and down the banks, chopping with quick, snakelike strikes at the brush, making a curving swath up the bank, then turning abruptly and chopping back down to the gravel beside the road, thence to leap onto the road and look to the guards for a sign of approval for his work. He would wipe his brow, inhale several times, blowing his cheeks out as he exhaled, then repeat the performance hour by hour. The preacher kept a close eye on his small companion as he hacked along, not getting as much work done as most of the others, but enough that the guards didn't complain.

The days wore on and on. Balky vaguely realized that the long-termers, bent silently to their punishing tasks, diminished his own semi-toughness. He was an interloper, a transient, a brief wayfarer through their long trek, their unending days. Yet he had a status of sorts; he had fought the law, their sworn enemy, and an enemy of their enemy was their friend. Of sorts.

A short-time misdemeanant, Balky was a step-brother. But they taught him to see that he had a habit of nervous, inane chatter, and they broke him of that. No hand was ever raised against him; it was the way their slow, troubled eyes turned from him. Their rejection was a denial of his existence. If they called out for water, he would rush to them, anxious to enter any conspiracy that would enliven the days, to whisper furtively out of the corner of his mouth, to let them roll a cigarette from his tobacco if they would only ask. But they never did. They would plunge the dipper into the water, take a mouthful and swish it around in their mouths to take the dust out, spit it upon the ground, then drink a full dipper. It was as if a machine had brought lubrication to another machine. Never once did they seem to notice that it was Balky Guffin who brought water.

Then there was an abrupt change in the preacher's attitude toward Balky. Although he had continued to make oblique reference to him in his cellblock sermons, he now began to smile at Balky when he brought water. When Balky ladled out the beans and fatback at mealtime, the preacher would say, "Thankee, neighbor," in a manner that caused Balky to shrink. It was close contact with the preacher that was so frightening. If one were removed, both physically and emotionally, one could maintain a sense of amusement. During evenings in the cellblock, the preacher began to close in on Balky, a slow, deadly stalk. Normally Balky sat on his bunk reading from his supply of paperback books, but his demeanor suggested that he was willing to stop reading and chat if anyone cared to do so.

The preacher prowled about with feigned preoccupation while the others wrote letters, worked at their leathercraft, or stared into the horrendous landscape beyond the walls of their minds. His meandering stroll always brought him near Balky's bunk area. The preacher's method was suddenly to stop, turn his head, and stare fiercely at Balky as if to plumb the fathoms of his heart. It was both alarming and a small, hopeful sign to Balky. Maybe an opportunity was coming for a bit of understanding and some interesting talk. Despite the wild preaching, Balky felt that in a sane, collected conversation the preacher would be able to talk about Biblical matters. Balky was not unversed in the Good Book. Perhaps they could find a common ground. One night he chanced it. The preacher had made his lumbering prowl up and down the cellblock, eyeing Balky. He had his Bible tucked under one arm and slowly stroked his beard with the other hand. When he drew near, Balky looked up, smiled, and asked, "How are you getting along, Reverend?"

It startled the preacher. He stopped, stared, then recovered and dragged his chains quickly to Balky's bunk. He stared with demon eyes, a hideous grin under his flaring red beard. His teeth were dirty.

"I'm doin' jes' fine, brother, and I hope the Lord has been treating you well. I been meaning to get around to seeing you. I wanted to see if you was ready to meet the Lord. Ever' chanct I git I witness fer the Lord. I guess you noticed.

"Now brother, it is a fact we have been put on this earth to give glory to God and to manifest his works at ever' chanct. I like to show any man who ain't met the Lord the way into the Holy House where abideth Him forever and ever," he said. He nodded slowly and thoughtfully, and two red craters studied Balky, weighing his reaction. A moment of silence passed: everyone in the cellblock watched without looking. Balky was flustered, sought for the right word.

"Say. How is it they let you set up that tent . . . er, ah, that tabernacle back there?"

"Why, I jes' told the captain that I needed a place to pray in privacy, and a place to lead the lambs home. That's how."

"Yeh? Is that what you do in there?"

"Yes it is. Don't you ever doubt it, either." He slapped the thick Bible.

"Now brother. I been sent here by the Lord especially for the likes of you. 'Course we are all sinners, but I can tell that you have been somewhat looser than most. It is the Lord in Heaven's desire that you put yourself under my guidance . . ."

Anger flashed on Balky's face, but he shook it off and tried again to reach common ground.

"Reverend, does your Bible there have the Apocrypha?" he asked.

"What? What is that?" the preacher demanded suspiciously in a shift of mood, tilting his head.

"Why, the apocryphal books, the unofficial books," Balky said, suddenly wary.

"No," the preacher roared, glaring wildly. "I never heard of no sich apockaficikal books. What are you? A jew or a catholic or something?" Then he grinned wickedly and swung his face around the cell. Now everyone was watching openly—noncommittal—except for the cretin parishioners who waited near the stove and snickered uneasily.

Balky reddened at the reaction his question had evoked.

"No? But I know you've heard of the Apocrypha. The books of Esdras and of Tobit, of Judith? Ecclesiasticus? The Hymn of the Three Holy Children, the Maccabees . . ."

"No! No! By all that's holy. There's no sich books in the Holy Bible. You're a-lyin', feller. Thar's nothin' writ like that in God's Holy Word."

He turned and stalked away, his fury radiating through the cellblock. He thumped his Bible down on his bed, knelt to enter his tabernacle.

So! thought Balky, his lower jaw struck forward aggressively. He knows nothing.

In the following days Balky approached the preacher several times, willing to discuss the Scriptures and to try to make whatever compromises would defuse the wild hostility in the preacher's eyes. But the preacher refused to talk, nor would he answer any questions on any subject. He would grab his Bible, glare murderously at Balky, then chant from the speckled pages in powerful tones of accusation. Balky now knew that he was a major threat to the preacher. He represented the fearsome and mysterious freemasonry of education—a brotherhood that the preacher would never enter.

Balky, being a native mountaineer, had read and studied the Bible extensively. A man is driven to it in self-defense if he is raised in that grim and foreboding fundamentalist territory. But at the same time, he did not care to read any more into it than it held for his mind at any given state or stage of growth. As he thought of the preacher, his anger grew and spun off silent arguments against the many old ignorant preachings and superstitions he had heard all his life. He refused to accept the sins of his father, for instance; in fact, he had never been sure what *sin* meant. He did not know if he were tripping down a rose-strewn path to perdition, but fear would never hold him back. He had his own ideas. He'd rather burn in hell than choke his mind and soul on worthless prescriptions for salvation dispensed with such ease by spiritual con-artists like this red-bearded preacher. No, he would not be waylaid by questionable religions or shackled by narrow chains of doctrine dreamed up in some phlegmatic, delirious head. Yes, yes, he declared to himself, there is a God, there is a spiritual plane, and there is a church, but it is invisible to most eyes and few have seen it.

Balky Guffin held unequivocally to the position that each man is entitled to his own misunderstanding of God.

The split widened. Balky lay low, considering the preacher's apparent physical strength and his following among the convicts who gathered with him. The preacher no longer tried to get to Balky, except for insinuations during his more agitated sermons. The true followers made snide remarks, heavy with ganged threat. Balky realized that if it were up to the preacher, neither repentance nor anything else would suffice to get him into heaven. Just as well. If he had to share paradise with imbeciles, he would take a running go at hell.

His days grew lonelier still. Those in the cellblock who weren't actively for the preacher weren't even passively for Balky. Yet it was helpful that the preacher couldn't mobilize everyone in that long room of men accumulating hellish time, that long shed of outcasts and social rejects. Often Balky lay on his bunk and considered the shrunken, oppressive universe that the chaingang had become. He watched the preacher without seeming to watch, seeing that the preacher was like an intuitive, frightened janitor alone in a huge plant of dynamos and grinding machinery wired to hate, passion, greed, murder, and other dark, electric forces. The preacher constantly sought another to entice, to counsel with, yet he was uneasy lest he touch a sensitive switch or fuse and unleash the power of that gathered hostility. He intimidated with his Bible only those he had carefully sounded out. And to those helpless, pitiable few he was a voice, giving words to their fears, sorrows, angers, resentments.

His muttering against Balky increased, and when the younger man was near, his eyes rolled about in visible hate. A sense of foreboding fell across Balky. For days on end, he moved about depressed, waiting for he knew not what.

At its best, the cellblock held danger. Most of the men had a knife hidden somewhere. Balky grew more afraid, and at night he entered sleep uncertain of seeing the dawn. He sensed a ghostly presence like a wild beast prowling the cell. If a man will be murdered and knows it, there is some slight consolation in thinking that the killer will pay. But Balky knew that if the preacher killed him, not one man would violate the cellblock's dark ethic and name the killer. One day he remained in the cell on sick call. He was alone. After the doctor left, he took out a metal bunk slat and honed it to razor sharpness on the concrete floor.

Balky's fear fed his curiosity. He morbidly tried to discover something about the preacher's crime. But no man knew, or said.

Woodrow! But if Woodrow even spoke to anyone, the preacher's eyes slitted and fire ran in his brain until he learned what Woodrow was saying. Balky developed a strange compassion for Woodrow, the pale little man whose discolored and twisted arm was like the roots which grew out of the road banks where they worked. His physical ugliness had at first repelled Balky, but he had come to practice those spiritual mechanics which accepted all ugliness as a part of existence and therefore beautiful. Generally one learns from grotesques. There is a higher law of compensation: if one has been short-changed in one purse, it is made up in another. Yet despite all, it seemed that Woodrow had been slighted in every account by nature's auditor.

One night as the preacher preached, Balky saw Woodrow cast a hopeful eye toward him, as he washed his socks in the sink at the end of the cell. Balky saw possibilities. Woodrow's eyes were hooded and turned to watch the preacher deep in his message. He began to move slowly toward Balky, softly, lest the chains clink. Curiously the gathered cult watched Woodrow. But the preacher did not notice.

Woodrow reached Balky and cut his eyes toward the preacher. He clutched his hand and whispered: "Listen, I know ye're my friend. I know that. I can tell. I got to say this: I

didn't do nothin' to get put in prison fer. No indeed I didn't.
All I wanted wuz to find peace and do the Lord's work and be
good. He got me into . . ."

His small, pinched lips trembled. "Hit were the preacher! I
were his gittar player in the church, an' . . ."

Suddenly the various small noises of the cellblock had ceased
and the silence was heavy. The voice fell the length of the
center aisle like a giant oak falling.

"Woodrow! Git here to this tent."

And something was revealed in that cellblock darker and
more oppressive than imaginable. Woodrow's face lost its confused hope and went even grayer, more desolate. It was the face
not of one imprisoned, but of one released into brief hope, then
recaptured. His chains clinked and clanked as he made his way
back up the floor. Every eye was upon the small, bent figure.
He entered the tent with the preacher and paid in long, drawn
silence. Balky watched without the courage to intervene. Afterward, the preacher emerged quickly and stood in silence,
beaming rays of deep hatred at Balky from wild eyes. Balky
was more frightened than he had ever been. There was nowhere to turn for help. The preacher seemed to be in control.
Prison authorities deferred to him, perhaps with the hope that
his services would hold down disciplinary problems.

Then Balky's honor-grade privileges were expanded. Each
evening he accompanied a guard into Murphy in the mail
truck. His time was spent outside the preacher's influence. He
was allowed to stay outside the cellblock for longer and longer
periods after he returned from Murphy. He remained in the
kitchen drinking coffee with other trusties, ran the bloodhounds for exercise, or jogged through the woods to the river
to fish. Usually he went to the cellblock only in time to retire
for the night. Some nights he risked a glance toward the tabernacle and the burning eyes of the preacher, like those of a copperhead waiting under a rock ledge.

Soon he got to make the run to Murphy without the guard—

with unanticipated results. A young blonde in a little car offered her companionship. He wasted only a moment contemplating the penalties. She pressed it upon him, and he could
find nothing wrong with getting his locks shorn. Yea, verily,
he thought, pushing his hair back and heading toward her.

She was a kitten, uncertain of her charms ... in a small town
with little choice of suitors who knew the arts of romance.
What could be lonelier? They met each evening for weeks.
Sometimes Balky thought of the sterile existence of the felons,
even as he lay in the throes.

But not often.

The guards never caught on to his nightly pursuits, or if
they did, they never let on. But the preacher knew. From some
deep and sour instinct he knew. He divined that Balky had
been with woman.

One night Balky returned early. The cons were busy with
their crafts or were sunk into their blank, listless meditations.
The preacher waited until Balky sat on his locker, then he
moved toward him.

"Ye've been layin' up with a woman, aincha?" he demanded.
His eyes glittered. His glance spiked into Balky's soul like
fangs.

"Yes, ye have. By all that's holy. A violation of Christ's own
kingdom. The temple that ye've been trusted to keep clean
and untouched by sich sin as 'at. I can tell. There's a clear
distinction between a man that's had a woman and one that
ain't. Yas! A great difference, and you, blasphemer and forni-
cator, have broken not only the camp rules but the Lord's own
ordinances."

Balky leaped up, nervously rubbing his palms over his trou-
sers. He glanced about at the stony faces of the men who
watched without watching. He detected a shrewd speculation
in their eyes now. He had never felt the power of their un-
spoken feelings more. Perhaps it had been the reference to
camp rules that had caused their wariness. Any mention of

rules was immediately suspect. The preacher caught their reserve, and he lost some of his force.

"Oh, I'll not tell the cap'n," he said, "but boy, if you value your soul you'll listen to the preacher now. You'll come to salvation, son. You'll wash yourself in the blood of the Lamb and fling yourself in fear and trembling at the foot of the Master's cross."

His voice was gurgling and hissing, and the bony, vulgar hand stretched out, palm up, and hinged back and forth slowly on his wrist. With the worn blandishments, now given power by the underlying threat in his husky pleadings, he tried to draw Balky into the mysterious tabernacle.

"Come sinner, and repent. I can wash you clean. You'll have to pay in pain, the pain of the cross, all right, but you've soiled the Lord's own robes . . . Him that bled and died on the cross fer the likes of you. Leper, thar's hope; dog, thar's salvation even if you ain't worth it; pig, won't you listen now to somebody that knows? To someone who's been sent here by the Holy Ghost to bring you back into the fold? Come home, sinner, oh yes come home and I'll let you pay your miserable way back into the graces of the Lord."

The preacher's eyes shone with unearthly radiance, his beard bristled with strange electricity. His tapered, obscene fingers plucked about in the air as if to find the strings which would pull Balky into that grotto of cloth. The others watched silently. Woodrow sat on the wooden box at the foot of the cots he and the preacher used, his lips working soundlessly as he repeated the preacher's words after him.

"Oh no you don't," Balky said, his voice breaking in a terror that rushed up out of his subconscious. "You have no idea what you're saying." He watched himself from a distance and saw that his mind was almost too benumbed to resist. He felt the evil venom drain into his soul. He turned his head awkwardly and opened his locker top. For a long time he fumbled blindly in the box, afraid to look up. It was lights out when he finally took a shower. His body felt dirty and infected. It was the preacher's first encroachment into his soul. He did not know how to fight the invasion. Yet, a stubborn rebellion was building in him. He smiled grimly: it was plain now to see that the preacher would have none of his lambs reveling in the fleshpots of Murphy, North Carolina.

But it was spoiled for Balky and the girl. Balky's joy changed into remorseful brooding. His anticipation turned to dread. He was with her after the preacher's tirade, but it was no longer beautiful or even hot and urgent. Ringing in his mind were the preachments from that furious man.

"Yas, ye've soiled the Lord's own robes, Him 'at bled and died for you . . ."

The girl sensed that something had changed, that Balky was now sick in his own flesh. One evening she didn't show up. He never saw her again. Then Balky began suffocating in his own mind. He brooded and wandered about, depressed, no longer aware of the late autumn grandeur.

The preacher grew bolder. Each time Balky dished out the grub at lunch he found himself confronted. The preacher warned him again and again of his heathen condition. He quoted scripture as Balky ground his bush-axe on the stone, and he kept a close eye on him for any sign of weakening. The tabernacle awaited. Balky kept his face impassive, fearful that the preacher would see that he was sinking into a curious receptivity. But he held out and gave no sign.

Early winter came. For months Balky had suffered his doubts. One night he went for the mail and returned, filled with desolate memories of the blonde. Instead of hanging about outside, he went straight to the cell. The preacher was speaking to his group. Balky struck his toe on the leg of a cot.

"Goddam it," he said angrily.

The preacher stopped his rant, looked around, then bounded toward Balky.

"Thou shalt not take the name of the Lord thy God in vain,"

he rasped, his eyes ablaze and his beard bristling. Then as if an aneurism had filled and broken, Balky's anger flew forth.

"You better get off my back, preacher."

"I tell you, sinner, thou shalt not take the name of God in vain . . . sinner, you have stretched your luck . . ."

"Don't pull this on me, you son-of-a-bitch," Balky spat.

"You've done it now, blasphemer," the preacher shouted, coming at Balky with his fists doubled up. Balky met him. Strange, he had always expected the preacher to take him, but Balky laid him out cold with one right hook.

"You shut your goddamned mouth now," Balky screamed, "and don't ever open it to me again or I'll kill you."

By the time the guard looked through the bars, Balky was back at his bunk. The guard looked up and down the rows: for some reason the convicts stood each at the foot of his bunk, looking blankly at one another.

"Well, what happened? I want to know what happened?"

A lifer at the end of the cellblock spoke. "Uh. He fell down, Cap'n. He got carried away with his preachin' and fell down and hit his head on the box. He'll be all right."

"Well, get 'im up from there."

Everybody waited a moment, then two of them carried the preacher to the tent.

It was not a week later that the preacher's cap appeared behind the stove. It surprised nobody. After the fight, his voice was stilled. Only he and Woodrow went into the tent at night. The preacher lost his following, sat pitifully alone in the mess hall at night, except for Woodrow. At first the preacher's congregation came to Balky—not in anger, but humbly as if he had deposed the king and now must serve their needs. But they were ignored. When the preacher's cap went down, the cons rallied despite their feelings about him. Everyone put something in the hat. At lights out, the cap was filled with coins mixed with a few bills. The next afternoon, the preacher sneaked the coins to the canteen-trusty to swap for bills, so

he wouldn't be burdened with coins when he took his run.
That night he went into the latrine and shaved off his beard.
As he passed Balky's cot, he leveled a long, bitter stare at him.
Balky stared back in curiosity. The shave had exposed to the
world a tortured, harried man. He looked weaker. That night
as Balky waited for sleep, he heard a file cutting slowly on
leg chains. As sleep came, Balky had one fleeting, disturbing
thought. The next day was to be his last on the chaingang, and
it was also the day the preacher would probably make his
dash for freedom.

His last day was a rare, splendid treat. One of those days
that comes to the mountains perhaps once a winter, rousing
nostalgic images from the past. The sky was like heady wine,
a flagon of the deepest blue . . . biting champagne capped down
over jagged, smoky peaks. Each breath of the sharp air was
like a drink of the rarest spirits, unsettling and disquieting in
the same instant that it fulfilled. The sun pressed brightly out
of the crystal air; and the even balance of sun and chill was not
uncomfortable. Well-being pervaded each atom of Balky's
body and he knew that he would soon be free again. Then there
welled up within him suddenly an intolerable sadness. He felt
a kinship and brotherhood to the poor laboring devils who
must swing bush-hooks along the roadways of Cherokee County until age and death caught them with another grim scythe.

He worked through the morning at the grindstone, singing
softly to himself. He was accepted now and had promised to
kite many letters out past the guards when he was released.
From his vantage near the grindstone in the rear of the truck
he watched them working along the banks—swinging in their
easy rhythm—lift, chop, pull back the axe, lift, chop, pull . . .

The preacher worked harder than usual. When he felt Balky
looking at him, a deep embarrassment seemed to come over
him. Secretly Balky wished him well in his break and hoped
that he would get far enough to enjoy a few days of freedom.
He would not remain uncaught. That is a lie they tell them-

selves. But even a few days are worth a month in the black hole if one is building a lifetime at Peachtree.

Woodrow hopped up and down the banks, chopping with his own quick snake-strikes. He turned and saw Balky at the grindstone, then dragged his chains toward him. He came around from behind the little trailer, handed Balky his axe, and took a drink of water from the bucket. Balky ground one side of the blade, then turned to get a cigarette. He didn't see the preacher walk toward the back of the truck.

"Naw, I ain't a-goin' . . . I ain't a-goin'," Woodrow screeched. "Gimme 'at axe, fer God's sake, Mr. Guffin."

Balky turned in time to see the little gnome leap up and try to reach his axe. But the preacher was upon him, stabbing him in the sides and back with quick thrusts of a long knife.

"Hey preacher, goddam you," Balky yelled and leaped to the tailgate. Woodrow was on the ground, and the preacher bent quickly to his own chains, pulling them apart where he had filed them through the night before. He straightened, flung a bitter, vengeful glare at Balky. He threw the knife. The handle hit Balky's shoulder; the knife fell harmlessly. With a quick leap the preacher cleared a fence by the side of the road and was in an old cornfield, running.

"Goddam you, Reverend," Balky shrieked again and jumped from the truck to where Woodrow lay. The guards were simultaneously covering the other cons and blasting their loads into the cornfield. From his crouched position over Woodrow, Balky could see the preacher running through the withered fodder left on the stalks, and buckshot blasting it down all around him. Balky lifted up Woodrow's head, then his shoulders, and through the slashed shirt he could see the deep red slits in his flesh like big fish gills. Blood welled out and Balky turned him over. The shotguns and 30–30s stopped blasting.

"Is he dead?" Woodrow asked, trembling.

"I don't know, man. But he's down. That son-of-a-bitch. How do you feel, Woodrow?"

Two guards were herding convicts past them into the truck. The cons looked regretfully at Woodrow.

"Lissen, ah'm gonta die. I kin feel it creepin' up on me. He shoved 'at blade through ever'thing I got in me."

Even then the mutilated organs began pumping the last of his blood out the slits in his side.

"But you done it last week. Good. Thar when you knocked him on his ass. I felt like you run the devil hisself outta my body. I felt free, and say, I heerd the preacher talkin' to hisself all that night, and he cried some, too. H'it were awful."

He coughed and fell silent. Balky tried to staunch the blood by pressing his hands against the wounds. He wanted Woodrow to live, but he knew that he wouldn't. Woodrow reached his twisted claw to his shirt buttons and tried to open the shirt, but Balky anticipated him and unbuttoned it. On his chest was scar on top of scar—little stab wounds all over his chest. Most were of recent infliction.

"There, you see," Woodrow whispered, "he'd get me in thar and cut on me. Oh, how he liked to do that. He said it wuz how I could pay fer my sins. An' I wuddn't the onliest one, either. He said he wuz sent here by God to cleanse us of our sins 'at way.

"He was a mean man—meaner than the devil ever had time to be. Lissen to me . . ." His voice was losing its volume and speed, like a wind-up record player running down. "The things he done, he made me say I done 'em too. The judge said he orta put us both in the gas chamber, but the jury wuddn't let 'em, fer some reason. But I wuz jist his gittar player at them revivals he had, and I didn't even know whut he'd done until he got arrested and brought me into it. 'Twuz jist like him to make somebody else he'p pay fer his work."

Woodrow's voice had sunk to a whisper now. The convicts sat in the truck, watching and listening attentively.

"His sister sent her three daughters to stay with 'im . . . young girls, one fourteen, one twelve, and one not yit ten. He told 'em hit were God's will that they do what he wanted 'em to do. Hit went on fer six months, then they said they wuz gonta tell. The devil! He took 'em into the woods late one evening. I didn't know nothing about it. I stayed at his house cause he ast me to . . . "

He coughed and something else came loose inside him and more blood surged out. One more such cough would surely kill him.

"He beat 'em girls first, swelled ther eyes shut, the c'yaroner said, then he cut their tongues out and cut their throats and they died."

He searched Balky's face with hopeful eyes to see if what he had said had gotten through. "God bless ye, Mr. Guffin," he said, then spasmed in one last racking cough and the last of his life dribbled out. Upon his face was a brief expression of release. With a long sigh, his tortured and bedeviled soul passed into paradise.

The truck driver pulled the truck down the road a little way. The convicts sat, watching thoughtfully, quietly. In a while a hearse, a State Highway Patrol cruiser, and a Sheriff's Department cruiser rounded the bend in the road, lights and sirens going. The men hurriedly braked, got out and looked around, their few words hushed. The coroner examined Woodrow and said, "Bled to death." He looked at Balky, whose hands and shirt were covered with blood.

"No shit?" Balky said.

The coroner bent to Woodrow. "Those are wicked cuts. Who done it, another con?"

The gun-boss nodded his head toward the cornfield. "He's layin' over thar. You better have a little peek at him too."

"Oh? Is he dead too?"

"He could be. He's fulla holes and he ain't breathed in twenty minutes."

The coroner joined the men, and a skirmish line of deputies, guards, and state patrolmen advanced into the cornfield. They

bent, talked a moment, then the two ambulance men carried
the preacher back to the road in a wire basket. They put him
into the back of the hearse. Then they picked up Woodrow,
laid him on top of the preacher, and draped a sheet over both
of them.

Balky rose up from where he had knelt, tears in his eyes.

"Man, goddam," he said, "don't put Woodrow in there
with him."

The attendants looked at him a moment and shrugged, but
did not change anything.

"Not under that cloth together," Balky said softly to himself, except that the other convicts heard and nodded. "He
ought not to have to bear that on his way in," Balky said. They
nodded again.

Tears bleared his eyes and he looked down to where Woodrow had died. The blood had stopped steaming and lay in pools
with squirming minnows of coagulation forming.

All the cars wheeled around in the road, then the hearse. In
slow convoy, led by the truck full of convicts, they came
down the steep, curving gravel road out of the mountains.
Balky sat in the trailer with the guards, watching the swaying
convicts, who sat loosely, morosely, jolting in the rear of the
truck. The guards looked over the fields and woods, evading
the eyes of the convicts.

It was early afternoon, but when a con runs or is killed,
they take that squad in for the day. In the cellblock, the convicts sat on their lockers for a long time. Then a lifer got up
and went to the preacher's bunk. He ripped down the tenting.
He took one look at the tortured, leather Christ's head, hesitated
briefly as if in deep thought, then rolled everything up and
handed it to Balky. Balky went to the stove and stuck the
bundle into the flames. The convict got the big Bible and
placed it gently on Woodrow's bunk. As the flames caught the
cloth, the stovepipe began rocking and jarring, and roared as
if a dozen demons were trying to flee to the sky.

Then the lifer went to Woodrow's bunk and carefully laid out his meager possessions. Along with the Bible, he put everything in Woodrow's pillowcase. Then he walked up the aisle very slowly—like a crucifer in the processional—and handed it to the guard. Each man sat deep in thought in the quiet cells of his skull. A deep wonder pervaded the vacancy in the cellblock, even as the guard called out:

"Balky Guffin. Get your stuff. You can go home this afternoon."

The High-Pitched Laugh of a Painted Lady

TRAPLINE TAYLOR WAS AT THE HARDEST part of his work: cleaning and racking the furs in the pole shed at the east end of his line. He was down now to the mink, and the skinning was easier. At midmorning he had begun heating the tub of water. As soon as it boiled, he had put in several spruce boughs and lowered his smaller traps into the water to kill the scent of his hands. He spent the remainder of the morning sitting in the door, from which he could throw the skinned carcasses down into the laurel on the steep slope beside the shed.

At noon he glanced toward Walker's Gap because he sensed a subtle change in the temperature—and because all the weather for this valley was made beyond the gap to the southwest. He saw only a small bright rim of cloud showing through the notch in the big mountain ridge. He took his traps from the tub and hung them to dry. By midafternoon the clouds were building higher and higher over the gap, but there was no wind to spread them through the sky. Another hour brought a small but brief stir of wind, colder than he ever remembered a breeze to be.

He knew it would come fast and it did. Big wind. Cold. The wind took the full, rounded clouds and dragged them across the sky at high altitudes until they were ragged streamers. Then the wind shifted enough to thin the streamers and patch them together with long, looping slurs until there was a high overcast, dimming and bending the sun's rays.

Trapline had spent most of his fifty-odd years in this section of the Western North Carolina mountains. He knew that the storm's main force would come with the second layer of clouds—clouds that would come in low and fluffy so that the underbelly of the storm would rip open on the notch and spew snow and ice and freezing winds across the valley. He knew it would be a fierce son-of-a-bitch, a big mean dog with teeth of frozen silver that meant to stay and hunt awhile and kill as it pleased. He had seen only three or four such storms in these mountains, but he knew there was going to be hell to pay.

Trapline stretched the final mink hide over the wire rack, then began to inspect the weasel furs. He was the last man known to be skilled enough to take the weasel by trap. One pelt was torn where he had skinned it wrong, so he threw it to his two cats. Those cats would fight over every scrap of every animal, except one. They wouldn't touch bobcat meat.

Trapline cleared the shed rafters of cured furs and placed the new skins at random on the poles. The poles were racked up just under the shed roof so that the skins could get the sun's heat without getting its rays. He looked once more at the sky. Angry dark clouds were shifting here and there like muscles moving under the hide of a great beast. He measured his firewood, hurriedly carried in more. He put kindling on the coals, then wood, and blew up a flame. He went back out and looked at the gap in the distance. Seven miles, more or less, to McKinney's filling station on the highway that ran through the gap. The wind whipped, snarled at the corner of the shed. He decided to try it. His livestock at the big cabin at the other end of his trapline hadn't been fed for two days.

He got his big coat, stuck the sawed-off .22 rifle under his belt, put a knife and a waterproof container of matches in his pocket. Then he looped the stake rings of a pair of No. 2 traps and hung them around his neck, thinking vaguely that he might have enough time to set them along some drain.

Trapline set out jogging down the ridge and, even as he went, felt the air turning much colder. After a mile he stopped. His breath was visible. He sat a moment, but the ground was too cold to rest on now. All he could see through the notch of Walker's Gap was blackness. The first flakes of snow swirled about like strange white bees.

Only a little of the storm was passing through the gap. It was as if the high ramparts of the mountains acted as a dam, holding back the main strength of the storm. He ran again until he could see the black wedgelike shapes of the big red spruces that grew on the spine of Walker's Ridge and on its long slope toward the gap.

Just then the storm sprang across the mountain, and at the same time darkness fell. But as the snow swiftly covered the ground, a half-light came off the earth and he made out his landmarks easily enough. He had run these mountains for many a year, and his eyes were so night-sharp that he could have seen landmarks on the afternoon of the Crucifixion.

He began to tire, but he still had a good piece to travel before he reached McKinney's station. McKinney would stay open if he thought some traveler might be stranded in the storm. Trapline wanted crackers and sardines and a place to rest before going on to his big cabin. The trail grew slick, and once he pitched down through a thicket of laurel and addled himself. He crawled back to the trail, half-crazy, and sat in the snow, shaking his head to clear it. When he got unsteadily to his feet, he was unsure of his direction. But the snow had not quite covered his tracks; he could see the way in which he had been heading and resumed his walk.

The storm was rising and howling when Trapline stumbled numbly onto the highway about two hundred yards below McKinney's station. Outside lights were burning, and through the swirling snow he saw three men moving about. For a moment he thought that they were closing the station.

"Hey!" he shouted. His lips were too numb. Suddenly he realized that his feet were freezing and that his hands were without feeling. His voice was lost in the wind. The men took no notice. He made his feet move again and ran on, holding a hand out before him to break his fall if he slipped or his legs locked. Finally he got within hearing distance.

"Hello! Hey! McKinney! McKinney!" he shouted. It was a lot of words for Trapline to use at one time. The men turned.

"Don't close," he shouted and ran on, but none of the men was McKinney. They were strangers, dressed for cold weather in the city, not for cold in these hills. They did not move to meet him, but as he stumbled into the light they looked at him intently.

"My God," one said, "what are you doing out in this weather? You look like a snow man."

"It caught me," Trapline said through clenched lips. He saw four cars covered by the deepening snow. That was more cars than McKinney usually saw on a good night. Two were new A-Models and one was a new Chevrolet coupe.

He went inside, stood just past the door, and stomped the snow off his boots. He tried to distinguish McKinney, but his eyes roamed the room vainly. Several men and two women. He could not take a close look now, but the after-image of one of the women remained with him and excited him. In a moment he glanced at her again. She had almost as much age on her as

he had, but her face was covered with a combination of red
and powdery white makeup that fascinated him. His eyes still
felt almost frozen, and they kept blurring. McKinney's wood
stove was red-hot, and a large stack of firewood was piled
against the wall. The top sticks still had snow on them, so he
knew that they had been brought in within the past few
moments.

He moved closer to the stove and opened his coat. The traps
swung free on their chains, then settled against his thighs. The
clanking broke the silence of the people.

"How far have you come in that weather?" one man asked.

He looked at the painted lady. She was staring at him with
interest. Something stirred within him. He moved his lips and
jaws, but the cold, followed by the sudden heat, made movement painful. He took off one of his work gloves, pointed to
his mouth, and grunted. Everyone laughed except one man
and the two women. He did not resent those who laughed or
those who did not laugh. He simply noticed everything, but
acted as though he had not.

Finally his voice came. He asked where McKinney was.

"Who is McKinney?" a man asked.

"He's the proprietor," another answered.

A man wearing a good leather jacket leaned against the
corner of the counter. "He's in the back room trying to find
some liquor," he said.

Trapline was silent. McKinney always kept some jars of
liquor to sell, under the counter.

"Likker?" he asked. "Does he keep likker here?"

"Well, I certainly hope he does," the painted lady said and
gave a high-pitched laugh. "It looks like we're going to be
here awhile."

McKinney burned only two dim bulbs inside the station,
but after the blackness outside, they seemed bright to Trapline's eyes. The electric lights began to flicker and sizzle. They

blinked out for half-a-minute just as McKinney came from the back carrying a half-gallon jar of whisky and a kerosene lamp. He went behind the counter and set the lamp and whisky down carefully. Then he saw Trapline.

"Howdy. Where did this catch you?"

"T'other end, skinnin' 'em out. I seed h'it a-comin'. I lit out fer y'ar. I hoped ye'd be open."

Trapline stared at the jar. McKinney looked at him significantly, then shrugged. The others crowded in. The painted lady pushed delicately, helplessly against the circle of people. Trapline watched her, and for a moment their eyes caught. She smiled, a quick flash, then the helpless look returned.

"Where are the glasses?" a man asked.

"Where is the five dollars?" McKinney asked. Trapline nodded slowly to himself. A jar usually cost two dollars.

There was a good-natured scurry to get up the money. A man laid it on the counter.

"Here is seven dollars," he said.

"I don't want but five," McKinney said, shoving two dollars back. "And there h'ain't no cups."

"How do you expect us to drink it?" another asked.

"Would you agree to let this good man who makes his living trapping animals show you how?" McKinney asked.

"Yes, yes," several said together.

McKinney handed the jar to Trapline, who slowly screwed the top off, stuck his nose to it and sniffed, coughed, and then drank. The others stared as he kept drinking. Finally he pulled the can down, breathed deeply. "Good 'erbs," he said courteously. Then he held out the jug to the painted lady.

She smiled awkwardly and said, "Not now. Somebody else go first."

One of the traveling salesmen took the jar from her, held it up to the light, and stared at it.

"Whew!" he said. "He took more than a pint."

The others murmured and laughed.

"Maybe he ought to pay for some of it," the other woman said.

"Good God, no," the man said. "He looks like life treats him hard enough without having to pay for booze."

McKinney looked at Trapline, trying to see him from the strangers' perspective. He had bought a lot of furs from Trapline over the past twenty years. They had been prime skins and brought good money. Trapline must have accumulated some wealth by now, because he never spent much except for liquor twice a year—once to celebrate the end of the fur season and his misery; and again to mourn the beginning of the next season. He bought his traps and chains at McKinney's when McKinney had them in stock, and he bought his food in town.

The others sipped at the jar. Soon an early glow was on them, and they bought soft drinks to chase the liquor, and then they began to take heartier drinks.

McKinney leaned over the counter and whispered to Trapline:

"I just got a half-gallon. I don't know them. They all come driving up with the storm. They might say something later to the wrong people. Yeh, and they might get drunk and do something crazy."

Trapline nodded. The caked ice and snow on his clothes had melted and the water was wetting him, but the alcohol had inclined him toward good will. McKinney lit two more lamps and set them in the back of the room so he could watch his merchandise. The wind began to blast, rattling the windows and shaking the walls. The lights flickered. The door burst open and in rushed the men Trapline had first seen outside. Their faces were frostbitten. They stumbled to the stove.

"Did you get the magneto fixed?" someone asked.

"No, hell no. I can't do it in this weather. We'll have to wait for a break. Is that likker I smell?"

They were handed the jar, which held less than a pint now. The first man drank about half, and the rest was split between the other two. Then every eye turned to McKinney, who shifted his weight from one foot to the other, discomfited.

"All right. Can you get us some more?" one asked. Two men were almost drunk. Three more were loud. The others were feeling good but no one could tell how good, or what direction their moods might take.

"No!" McKinney said. "No more!"

Trapline stared impassively at the strangers, who began to lower themselves to the floor near the stove. The room grew quiet except for the creaking of roof timbers and the buzz of the electric lights. But outside, the storm maintained its energy. The wind blew and lay back, and blew again like a great angry beast. McKinney's outside light still burned so that he could check the deepening snowfall. Trapline stood near the frosty window now and watched snow pile up steadily. When the wind gusted, the snow came in sideways out of the southwest; when the wind was down, it fell in great globs, building up layers quickly.

As he watched, Trapline thought about his stock and became uneasy. One of the least-drunk men asked McKinney how long he thought it would snow.

"Ask ol' Trapline thar. He's been out in these mountain weathers for many a year. He knows better than me."

They turned to Trapline. He went to the door, opened it, and stepped outside. The snow was thick in the air now, and it quickly coated his clothing. Light seemed to spin from the great winding fall of the flakes. He got a feel of the air and the wind, then went back inside.

"H'it'll clear sometime atter while, afore daylight. But h'it'll be colder'n Billy Hell," Trapline said.

Silence. In a while a man spoke.

"What is it you do? Run a trapline? What's a trapline?"

"Well sir, I go along creeks and springs and see where critters are a-nestin' or a-runnin', and I set traps and cotch 'em," he said.

"See where *who* is nesting, for God's sake?" asked the painted lady in a high, hoarse, and denigrating tone; then she laughed.

"By god, varmints!" Trapline snapped. "You understand that, don'che?"

"Yessir," she said meekly and looked at him.

Trapline continued. "Mink, muskrat, possum, coon, weasels . . . one time I cotched a otter and now I wisht I hadn't. I know where some beavers are and I won't set a trap in a half-a-mile of there. They is pretty and ain't many left."

"Well, good man," one man said, "what do you do with them when you cotch them, as you say?"

"Skin 'em and sell the hides," Trapline said.

There was mild interest in the conversation.

"Are the animals good to eat?" the man asked.

"I've eat some of all of 'em at times. Depends on where y'are and how hungry ye be. Muskrats is as good as wild turkey at the right time. Call 'em swamp rabbit. Weasels taste like cat meat, and I'll tell you one thing right now, cat meat ain't worth a damn for nothing. Ain't no way ye can cook it right."

"Well, I'll be double-damned," the man said, shaking his head. "Where do you sell the hides?"

"Right here," said McKinney proudly. "I'll show you some of his'n. He's the only one does it for a livin' anymore. Some people bring in hides during hunting season, but they don't run a regular line."

He went to the back room and returned with several limp furs and two on a rack. He handed them around. The men smiled and felt them. The painted lady rubbed the pelts and smelled the fur. She rubbed one skin against her face and smiled at Trapline.

"You say a number of people do this?" the man asked.

"No, no," McKinney said. "Numbers of 'em piddle at trapping, but nobody is as good at it as Trapline. Hell, he gets good prices because he tans a lot of hides too. Them thar that ain't been stretched out has been tanned. I pay more fer 'em and the company pays me more fer 'em. Most people trading in skins now damages the pelt at the traps, or else they cut it raggedy in skinning or stretching it. Then they can't get good money for it. Trapline y'ar gets top dollar."

Trapline looked at the floor in modesty.

Now the talk fell away to low conversation among various groups. Trapline stood near the stove until the legs of his pants had dried and turned stiff, then he moved near the counter. McKinney talked to him in a low voice. "They's four jars at the middle post in that sign down the road thar. I'll need fer ye to bring me one in a minute."

Soon the painted woman said, "Damn, I'd like to have a drink."

The others agreed. McKinney smiled. Trapline peered from beneath his floppy hat, his eyes almost hidden.

"All right, now. All right," McKinney said. "Trapline knows where to get some. But it's a hard trip for him. I wouldn't ask him to go in this weather, myself."

The painted lady laughed in hearty, hoarse sophistication.

"A good Saint Bernard is worth his weight in gold," she said. "How much would we pay?"

The others fidgeted, exchanged glances. Then one of them began to take up money. He got twenty-three dollars and brought it to Trapline.

"Can you get us a full can like that other one for this much?"

Trapline looked at it awhile. "Maybe so," he said. He hoisted his two traps onto the counter and went out. The snow had not abated. He walked straight to the billboard, groped in the snow, and found the liquor. Beating the snow from the lid of a jar, he unscrewed it and took a long drink. He put that jar back and took another one from the snow for them.

This time they measured up drinks in their empty soft drink bottles so that everyone could drink at his own pace. They bought more soft drinks. While they drank, Trapline gave McKinney five dollars for the jar, and they split the remaining eighteen dollars. Trapline used some of his money to buy several cans of fish.

Trapline dried his clothes again and sat behind the counter. He was hidden from the others, but he could listen to their talk and watch the woman. He listened also to the storm. The wind was rising again, and he heard ice instead of snow on the panes. He knew that the wind was blowing the sky clear now and making the air bright and cold. He curled up and slept, though it was chilly so far away from the stove.

He awoke before daylight. McKinney had kept up the fire most of the night, but he was sleeping now. The others sprawled about, snoring drunkenly. Some of them were pressed together for warmth. He was gratified to see that the painted lady had slept near the other woman. If he had his way, he would have her in his line cabin curling up with him.

Trapline chunked the fire. He did not eat the food he had bought. Soon McKinney got up and fried some ham and eggs, which he shared with Trapline. They did not speak until Trapline went to the door.

"Be careful. That's sheet ice now. When you get done, come back this way so I'll know you're all right and you'll know I'm all right. With this bunch stranded and scared, you can't ever tell . . ."

"All right. Keep pouring the redeye to 'em. That stuff can ca'm down a mad dog."

"Yeh man, or make a corpse start a fight."

They laughed at each other. The two traps were hung around Trapline's neck, and he buttoned his coat to keep them from swinging. He had taken only a few steps when he began to slip and slide. Then he broke through the stiff, stubborn crust. The snow was up to his knees. He realized that he was going to have a hard time getting to his other cabin. If he walked flatfooted he could stay on top of the crust, but it was too slick to make much headway. If he brought his feet down hard, the crust broke and at times sawed above the tops of his boots and chafed his skin. Dawn found him hobbling along—a dawn as clear and as cold as any he ever remembered, with high, shifting wind. His cheeks were numbed, and beneath the cotton gloves he felt the familiar cold burn of frostbite starting in his hands.

The bitterness of the day drove him to climb up Walker's Ridge so he could travel on the sheltered side. He gained elevation painfully and slowly, but finally the going became easier. The exertion warmed him, and the crust of snow was so thick higher up that it only bent with his tread. By the time he got to the spine of the ridge, the sun had brightened the sky but did not warm the air. The glare off the snow blinded him. He found an old twisted log dating back to the last forest fire and reaching under it, where the char was dry, he blackened his hand. Then he rubbed the soot over his cheeks and under his eyes, and looking again across the sunny snow, he saw that he had cut the glare by two-thirds or more.

As he crossed to the shaded side of the great ridge, the wind diminished to occasional gusts, which whistled and whispered around cliffs and hollow logs. He reached a small stream where he had set four traps. The first trap was in a laurel thicket. It had not been sprung. As he rearranged it, he realized that he was becoming too cold. He took dry leaves and old bark from underneath a low canopy of laurel and built a fire to warm his hands. Then he ate a can of fish, except for a portion that he put in the snow above the trap as a lure. Then he made a wide circle to go to the other traps. By then the chill was gripping him again, so he climbed back up the ridge a way and lay against a rock which was protected from the wind by trees. There he warmed himself, then continued homeward and did not bother to check the other traps.

His feet were now alive with a combination of pain and numbness, of cold and fire, and it was in his fingers too. He began jogging and walking fast to get to his place. By the time he reached the cleared slope above the cabin, he was falling and tumbling through the crust. The snow had blown in sideways, and his door was frozen so that he had to fumble to get it open. Then he fell inside.

The air was warmer but dense and bitter with the smell of dog droppings. The dogs came out of the back room whimpering, smirking, leaping on him, licking at the snow on his boots. He took off his coat, stiff with snow and ice, and threw it in a corner. He looked at his red claw of a hand as he felt for a match on the mantle. He lit the fire already laid in the fireplace, and before it caught good, he had his hands down to it. Soon the flames were high enough to make him back off. He added dry pine and oak and the fire took hold.

Trapline fell heavily to the floor where the new warmth from the fireplace reached him. He grinned to himself, once again the master of his fate, no matter what the weather held. The traps were still around his neck, and he shifted slightly for comfort. He warmed himself until the fire fell in. Now the dogs were whining and he got up, chunked up the fire, and fed the dogs, talking gently to them:

"Boys, she was hell comin' acrost Walker. If I try to talk ye into hunting that ridge anytime this week, tell me no . . ."

He thought for a moment of the painted woman.

"But if I go back that way tonight, don't try to stop me."

After the dogs were fed, he opened the door to air the cabin. He went to the sheds to feed the stock. He got the calves and cows into the barn and pulled some hay and fodder down from the loft for them.

Brute beasts! They did not hurry. Instead, they ate as though they had been fed every day. The dogs were leaping about on the crust, sniffing, uncertain about their scent but suspicious. They knew something. What? He saw no sign on the crust. A mule would have left no tracks on this glaze. He kicked open the frozen door to the chicken shed and saw his eight fowl packed together on the highest roost in the back of the shed. Something must have come for them and found the door iced shut. He sniffed the air.

Skunk? Mink? Weasel? Fox?

He got some feed, and taking the traps from around his neck, put them on the lid of the feed bin, outside the door. When he scattered feed across the floor, the hens and roosters came down to eat. He shut the door and tried to twist a piece of wire around the handle and the jamb to secure it, but it was a shackly old shed, with good-sized gaps in the walls. Usually, when he was home, the fowl roosted high in a pine tree behind the cabin.

He returned to the cabin and built up his fire. After cleaning the cabin, he stood on the porch awhile, feeling the weather. The wind had warmed a bit. He kept his eye on a ridge to the west until he saw what he was looking for. Fast dark clouds, moving in all directions. Another storm. Early flakes of snow came before it. He went in, lit a lamp, and ate from a can of fish. He watched the fire until it fell in on itself, then he heaped it high with wood, and it responded with a dance of flames to the windsong in the chimney. He curled tiredly on his cot and heard the hard snow peck at the window. He smiled broadly at leaping fire-images of land and sky and snow and wind and the half-drunk painted woman—and from there it was a short way to sleep.

He awakened slowly to the clamor. The dogs were barking and leaping at the door. The wind was fierce and shook the building, and in his half-awake state he thought that the wind was what had disturbed the dogs. He swung stiffly, reluctantly, onto the floor, then his bony shanks began to shake from the chill in the cabin.

The dogs quieted for a moment, though the wind was still strong. He hearkened to a tangle of noises beneath the wind.

Some loose shingles prying at their nails, a limb clacking against the corner of the house.

Then it came, something from the animals. It rose on dumb fear and came across the snow to him. A subdued gabble. He slipped on his clothing and shoes, found his flashlight, took down a Winchester from its rack over the mantel, and checked its loads. His dried boots, still hot from their place beside the fire, melted the snow crust as he stepped from the porch. The dogs raced about in circles, then together they homed on the poultry pen. He ran there and shined the light through the cracks. The fowl were packed up at the rear, the low gabble rising from them. Through the cracks he could see blood on the floor and some feathers. He held the Winchester in one hand and tried to untwist the wire with the hand that held the flashlight. It was useless, so he leaned the rifle against the feed bin where the traps lay. He finally got the wire untwisted, opened the door, and leaned through it. Though he was generally not surprised by anything the critters of the mountains did, he was not ready for the big bobcat.

It dropped out of the rafters from behind him and landed on his back. Claws spread wide and sharp, it climbed upward over him, screaming in wild catfear. Trapline too began to scream in fright and pain. The cat dug its front claws into the back of his scalp, and they went in to the skull. Its hind claws gave it the hold and strength to keep climbing. He smelled his own blood now. His dogs were leaping frantically about the door, unable to get past him to help. His sole thought was to back through the low door and knock the cat off. But he succeeded only in knocking it around to a more secure perch on his head. As the cat tried to climb again, the rear paws raked down through his forehead, slicing flesh so that it dropped completely over one eye, sealing it and covering most of the other eye. He felt the heat of the gashes, the frost in the air, the nearness of the cat. He lurched toward the feed bin, missed the Winchester, but felt one of the traps. In desperation he squeezed the shank of it until the jaws fell open. Then, twisting his body and pushing the trap upwards, he snapped the jaws on the bobcat's balls. The cat screamed once more and leaped from his head, spraying blood as it went. The stake ring on the trap's chain caught on a snag above the snow and jerked the cat to a halt. The dogs were upon it, ripping out its eyes and shredding its ears. In a moment the cat's guts were being tossed and dragged, steaming in the snow.

But Trapline heard nothing. He knelt in the snow, trying to feel the flow of blood so he could determine if any arteries had been cut. He knew that he was badly clawed, yet his thoughts wandered to how much he could get for the hide if the dogs didn't rip it apart. Finally he straightened, felt the fire of the cuts in his shoulder and back. He stumbled about in a small circle, suddenly very frightened because he could not see and he did not know whether his eyes were torn out or not.

He cursed and moaned, then dropped to his knees in the snow. He broke up the crust with his fists and flung himself face first into the snow to see if the cold would staunch the bleeding. He lay still and unseeing, trying to get his bearings by ear. He listened to the restless wind, its many voices—a cold stream of wind, a pushing army of wind, a prowling beast of it, a ripping point. And by these wind voices he was guided. He heard the low bulk of his cabin block the wind, heard the wind whisper as it flowed around the corners, its *ooofff* at the chimney. He rose and stumbled in the direction of the house, fell, flipped on his back, hands and arms instinctively covering his eyes and throat. Then he turned over and crawled to the porch. The cabin, its wood, its measurements were all of vast dimensions now that he was relying only upon the benumbed nerves of his fingers to instruct him. At last he got inside, shut the door, and fell beside the warm hearth.

Then for the first time in all the years of his manhood he felt a dark and hopeless grief well up and he wanted to cry. But he could not. It was as though the tear ducts had long ago atrophied and left him with no channel for grief if ever grief should arise. He choked on gall, held out his hands toward the hot stones of the fireplace. Slowly he let his head slump onto a bicep and he slept again.

He came awake later to one fact: he had a speck of vision in one eye. In the fireplace a chunk of wood had burned through and turned its coaled side toward him. He watched for a time until he could identify what made the glow. First he had been disturbed by its unremitting redness in a world of black, but his ears brought to him the slight sounds of slow burning and his heart leaped with hope. He turned his head and tried to look about, but he was sorer and tireder than he could ever remember being. So he let his head fall back on his arm, where he could train the small opening of sight upon the coals again. His hands were now warm and so was his face. He reached up to touch his eyes. The right one was closed tight—swollen and gashed. He touched the lid of the other one, found it much sorer, but took heart because even as it flinched and fluttered, the movement opened the lid a bit wider.

Now slowly his mind began to clear and he realized that he had slept again. For a time he did not stir—only listened, felt. The place was cold now. Some warmth radiated off the stones of the fireplace, but very little because the fire had burned for only a short time. He listened to the cold, lonely wind. It came at intervals, and when it gusted, he felt it. It was as if he could inflate himself until he occupied the total space of the cabin, then became the cabin itself. He marveled.

He turned and saw only a milky gleam of light. Then some objects came into focus in the crack of sight remaining. His fingers sought out the damage to his body. The blood had scabbed everywhere but a few places; it was still sticky in those. He could tell that his jacket and shirt had been shredded by the bobcat. His face was bruised below the claw damage, but that area was not in pain. He stood, found himself sore but able to walk, so he tottered to the table, fumbled about for another can of fish. It took him a half-hour to find the opener and get the can open. Once that was done, he got the last of the kindling and wood and built a fire in the fireplace, but even as it blazed up, he worried that the cabin would burn. He dug at the fish with his fingers and went time and again to check on the fire.

It came to him slowly that the wind was down. The silence was ominous. The motionless air, now grown strangely cozy and comfortable, told him that more snow would fall soon. He thought about it and decided he needed a doctor. His wounds would get worse if he was snowbound for several days. He might starve.

He searched about, groping awkwardly, until he found an old piece of wool blanket. With it he fashioned a crude poncho. He tried to fit his hat over the gashes, but it was too much. He ripped away part of the blanket and tied it loosely over his head. Then he banked the fire as best he could, opened the door, and went out.

He had not counted on one thing. Though the sky was overcast, there was still too much glare for his small crack of vision. He worried about it for a while, then noticed that his eye was beginning to adapt. He struck out slowly, moving along the barbed wire of his fence. When he reached the corner, he found that he could see another landmark, which would take him up the ridge. To follow the usual route to his traps would be shorter, but there the laurel and brush were so thick he would likely get lost. He began slowly to sidle up the snowy slope of the ridge. The dogs whined uncertainly, turned and looked at the warm cabin, then came with him. They fanned out on narrow flanking runs near him, sliding awkwardly where the snow was frozen, sinking up to their bellies where it was drifted. He guided himself by the blurry, distant ridge-line, sometimes catching a view of old fence posts, stumps, trees, rocks, before he stumbled into them—and sometimes not. Sooner than he expected he reached the spine of the ridge. He stood for a moment to rest and to try his vision. He could see the dark shapes of the trees near him on the ridge, but when he looked into the valley or across toward Walker's Gap, everything was pure white, disorienting him. He fretted, felt the dark anguish in his throat again. But he had to decide quickly because he was freezing. He pushed straight down the spine, and when he ran into the knotty trunk of one huge tree that he recognized, he realized that his direction had been right.

He tracked downward until he reached a flat, clear place. Determinedly he forced the left eye wider. The light pierced it like a hot needle, then the cold got to it. But he persisted until he could see enough of the bulk of Walker's Ridge across the valley to get a bearing. Then he sloped off the ridge to the east and immediately got into trouble, although he did not realize it until hours later when the shadows grew long. By now his dogs were no longer out on his flanks romping. They were trailing behind him, walking slowly with their heads and tails down.

He stopped and looked about. What he saw was not recognizable. It was almost dark. He should have found the highway long ago. Had he crossed it unknowingly? He could be lost forever. It was a long way through the mountains to the next road. He had no idea where he had gone wrong, therefore he could not rectify it. The dogs sensed his despair and came to him. He slipped off a glove and reached to the neck of one. Not much warmth coming from it. He cursed, wheeled, kept to that general direction, breasting into a sharp wind and new snow. His feet were burning slightly, then they lost all feeling for a time. When a little fire returned to them, he felt it also in his fingers and the sides of his hands and his face. For a time the prickle was unbearable, then it grew tolerable. He had suffered frostbite before, and now he knew it was going to be bad with him. Again he cursed, then he slowly grew quiet in his spirit and realized that the question of frostbite was moot. He might not live.

But if he must now fail, it would not be for lack of guts. That was the tradition of this land and the people. Even the danger of a dark fate lifted him above his exhaustion of moments ago. As darkness descended, his vision heightened because the glare was gone and he perceived the softest of blacks and whites. He moved along slower now, not out of tiredness but because he was caught up in the beauty of the snowy forest at night. He smiled, realized he had lived almost his entire life in the wilderness and had only a few times allowed the power and beauty of it to intrude and completely overwhelm him. Over the chill of the weather came the glorious and rare chill of realizing great beauty. His heart pounded in excitement at the thought of living—or dying—and at last, past midnight, exhilaration turned to quiet submission.

He climbed up a small cleared slope and fell heavily against a pole. The dogs came to him, and it was there that he began quietly trying to give up the ghost, to make those final preparations of spirit and soul. The dogs fell on him, curled, whined, buried their noses under their tails. He regretted that he had not kept more dogs. The warmth of more of them might have saved him. He reached to pet one. The snow was not so deep here. Something protruded. He scraped it out. A jar of whisky. He shook his head bemusedly, then without questioning fortune, he began trying to get the lid off. It took some time. He drank nearly a pint before he lowered the jar from his mouth. He set it in the snow beside him and belched quietly. He sat there for a time, then he heard a thin noise and strained his ears to hear it again. It was the high-pitched laugh of the painted lady. He smiled in secret pleasure. He felt now that he was dying, and he was not against entertaining the idea that she was one of the angels God would send to guide him home. He laughed aloud, and laughed and laughed. Then he heard it again. Perhaps it was closer. He did not care. It was the thing that could cause him to stop wanting to live. The painted lady.

She looked as if she had had her day, but still there was a great softness and sympathy to her, and those were the qualities he would expect of an angel sent to guide him in.

"Hell!" he muttered foolishly through his sliced face. "Hell, I'll go home in a pink buggy, by God," he said and reached for the jar to drink again. He sat upright. That was McKinney's liquor. He tilted his head and looked up. He sat directly under the signpost where he had gotten the whisky for McKinney the night before. Somehow he had lucked out. Even as his heart lifted with new hope, his shivering dogs raised their heads and looked at him.

Finally he stood, his bones and joints coldly creaking and snapping. He held an icy jar of whisky. By lolling his head back on his shoulders he gained some vision off to his left. With that he stumbled up the last embankment and onto the highway. The gap had remained snowed in. There were no tracks. To be sure of his position he turned himself so that he could bring the long bulk of McKinney's station into view. Yes, a blur of smoke wafted about the chimney above the white roof.

He felt born again. A new life. He would do better with this one. He was anxious to see the painted woman. Now he felt her womanness, stronger, warmer, than when he first saw her.

The woodsmoke guided him in as much as anything. His dogs yelped his trail, frisking about. At the door he began feebly banging with hard, blue fists. They did not answer immediately, and he leaned his swollen, gashed face against the wood. He could hear them murmuring, and somewhere in the noise he could hear a man and a woman drunkenly trying to sing. Now his numbness had gone, bringing a slow increase of pain. He felt ancient and decrepit, not wise but very child-like, and a tear came through the lacerations and he hoped the painted woman would come close to him or perhaps hold him for a moment.

She laughed again.

All of time manifested for him in that one instant, and he understood all things. Slowly he knocked again, as hard as he could, then leaned against the door. The voices ceased. Mc-Kinney opened the door and Trapline fell inside. The jar fell to the floor, slid along the planking, and stopped at the feet of one of the salesmen.

"Hello," he said. "It is the trapline man. He brought us some more good whisky."

McKinney was illumined by the strong light from behind the counter. He bent over Trapline.

"God damn, man. What have you tangled with?"

"Bah . . . bah . . . bah . . . cyot Bobcat. Bobcat. You hear? Clumb my back and went out the top of my head."

McKinney was examining the several coats of red lacquer on Trapline's shoulder. The others were coming slowly, stuporously, across the floor to see. Now Trapline felt the sudden heat of the place to be unbearable. Pain upon pain came to him, and from him, and radiated throughout the building. His ears began to ring, and he dimly realized that McKinney had let the hounds in with him.

He heard her. She raised her voice to falsetto. "Oh, is that our friend with the furs and traps? Whoopee! Did he bring us this whisky? Ah! He's drunk, too. Poor baby. I'll just kiss him."

Somewhere under the bloody gutters of his face a smile formed. He understood all things. Even a touch would be enough. He heard her feet on the planks. From a long way off she came, sounding down the labyrinths of time. Her laugh was gay—some would say a bit too highly pitched—but it did not offend him, muffled as it was by layers and depths of some substance he did not know. He smelled her perfume.

She knelt, pulled at him.

"Get up, old boy. You're a good old boy to bring us this booze. I just believe I'll give you a good smooch . . ."

Then she grew very silent, but he could tell the sound was building up. He felt her rise.

"He's cut all to hell," she shrieked. "Somebody has ripped him apart."

He heard her going away, back across the board floor. Her distance multiplied; he knew now that the heavy, muffling and distorting substance upon him was the very matter of time. Back there, eons away, near the stove, she shrieked and shrieked while one of the frightened salesmen held her. He felt the dogs pressing against him, heard McKinney coming with the whisky. Outside more hard snow began pecking at the windows.

The
Burial
of
Big Blue

T HE AUTUMN HAD BEEN MILD UNTIL THE
last of November, then winter stole into the mountains
hard and white. The first snow was not deep, but it was unex-
pected. The night before had been cold but clear. At dawn
the sky had filled with dark clouds, then the snow had fallen.
A few flurries still swirled about. Lon Clark arose, felt the
stiffness and aches of age. He knew immediately that snow
had fallen. He smelled the chill cleanness of it, felt it in the skin
on the top of his hands and wrists.

His wife got up soon after, complaining and bleating about.
He started the fire in her cookstove and one in the living room
fireplace. Then he went to the window beside the cookstove
and took up his watch on the ridge.

"You don't think," she said, "he'd be running any now, do
you? It's too cold fer it to work off."

"I don't know. I jist don't know. If he kept any heat at all
in or around his mash boxes . . . I've seen smoke up there since
October when the muscadines got ripe. Ummm, God! He'll
have brandy. Pure brandy."

"What he's gonna have is him and you back in the federal
pen. I've been worried sick ever since we seen that smoke. It's
been twenty-five years since he ran a drap. It's been that long
since you and him built six months' time fer the last batch.

You've not had a drap since, either one of you, have you? Well, answer me, goddam it," she said angrily—and clearly, even though she had not yet put in her false teeth. She usually let him have his way and his say, but when it came to liquor, then it came to trouble and he had no way of combatting her righteous anger. She had told him often enough about the hard time she had had when he went away. The force of her suffering was still upon them, even after twenty-five years.

Lon turned, looked at her. Smoke was rising off the frying fatback, and she had begun to sob quietly, flinging flour around, clouding the air in an effort to hide her feelings. He shook his head worriedly, stared back at the ridge where smoke had been wisping from Landon's place for several weeks.

"He'd have changed his run from grapes to apples in the middle of October, and I'll bet he's been running pure corn fer the past two weeks," Lon said.

"It is not your business, it is not your goddam business what he has been running. If I see or hear tell of you gitting with him on this, then I'm going to shoot you both. By God, I tell you, what I went through . . ."

"Now hesh, hesh, hesh, honey. That was a long time ago. Maybe he ain't makin' a-tall. Maybe he's jist burning something up there on the ridge . . ."

"No. Burning wood in that still. The old idjit. Goddam him. He made a good living off that farm after he got out of the pen, but he worried Berthy to death. She jist lived two years after the two of you got out. And she died hard."

"Well, what was it that made me usta think it was you and her who drunk up all that liquor we had hid when the damned law got to us that time? How come me to labor all them years under the idea that you and Berthy sold some of it and drunk up the rest?"

"Now it's your time to hesh, you old rooster," she said, a timid smile shining through her tears as she brushed back loose gray hair. "You jist shut up. All you got was hearsay and gossip. How come this is the first time you ever asked me about it?"

"Haw!" he cackled. "I was afraid it was the truth. Now you tell me, little darlin', jist what all went on while me and Landon was a-doin' our time?"

The coffee had perked. She sloshed a cup full and pushed it to him.

"I don't want to git beat or have somethin' throwed up to me from now till I die," she said, snickering. He poked at her ribs, raised the cup to his lips, and sipped loudly. But her mood swung abruptly.

"I don't want him down here. I don't want you up there. It's nothing but trouble," she said, sniffing sadly.

Less than an hour later, Lon looked out of the window and saw Landon weaving down the rutted logging road that led from his cabin. He wouldn't cut a proper road to his place because people from Florida were running up and down any road they could maneuver, trying to buy up mountain property. If anyone was set against them, it was Landon.

"He's coming. Sure as hell, he's coming," Lon said to himself. He was so old now that he never knew for sure whether he was talking to himself quietly or thinking too loudly, but he suspected that he muttered, much as his wife did. He edged into the bedroom, unloaded the shotgun and the 30–30 and hid them, then left through the back door and jogged stiffly to the shed. He was putting a shine on the edge of an axe with a file when Landon found him.

"Well, what in hell are you doin'?" Landon asked.

"Ah me. Hello, Landon. How you? All right? My arm and shoulder been givin' me trouble, and I was settin' out here where it's quiet tryin' to heal 'em up."

"Heal 'em up? It's thirty below zero and ice is caking up in west hell. You'll heal a damn sight sooner if you bake by the fire."

White stubble covered Landon's cheeks but failed to conceal red veins under the skin. He wore his coat underneath his over-all galluses. There was a great sadness in his face.

"Well, I see you're drunk as hell. How long has it been?"

Landon shuffled about, glancing here and there nervously. "How long has what been? Since I been sober or since I been drunk?"

For a moment both shook their heads, trying to understand the complexity of the question. Then Landon said, "I ain't had a drink of likker in about two hours. Before that it was last night since I had some. Before that I was makin' a little, but not drinking. Before that it was nigh fifteen years since I had a drap."

Lon looked at him sharply. "Fifteen year? I thought it had been longer 'n that."

"Yeh, you ain't drunk none since we got out of the federal, have ye? Do ye reckon I ort to believe that?"

"Well, I ain't, and I don't give a damn what you believe. How come you got to makin' again? You ain't hungry, are you? You don't need no money. You got more money than the banks have. They have to come up here to borry money off of you. I never seen a man with so much money."

"I got lonesome one day. My time is nigh. It is upon me. I jist wanted to see if I could still do it. I got my ol' still out of that cave in the bluffs, set her up, and fired 'er. I jist played fer a week or two. I mixed some hog shorts and water, acted like it were mash, and boiled it up in the still. I was like a boy playing. But you know what they say—a man that ever fools with a likker still will go right back at it someday. He can't stay away from a still. The next thing I knowed I was a-sproutin' a little corn and a-mashin' it and sourin' it and then a-runnin' it, and when the peaches hit the store I bought some, and I picked a lot of blackberries in their time, and when the muscadines ripened in the woods I set onto them—me and ol' Big Blue jist run the woods all summer and fall. I let them all sour in their tubs and boxes, then I run 'em. I had all that good stuff made there, jugged and jarred, so I set down and looked at 'er one day and I smelled and tasted 'er, and there went the whole shootin' match—drunk as hell ever since, and that's the full goddam story of my life, leaving out only a few incidentals here and there."

"You been busy all summer? Wheeoooo . . . I bet you got corn likker and good brandy up there from the apple and the peach and the blackberry and the grape, like no man ever set eye on before. You allus was the grandest one I ever knowed with a copper pot. I never met yore match. It was worth all the years we've been alive. It was worth six months of my time in the federal pen jist to have the honor of being raised up with you. Why, I allus said that a man could have a good time, even in jail, if he was with the right crowd. Yessir, I didn't mind six months in Atlanta as long as I had your pleasurable company."

"Don't start all that horseshit. I specially want you to shut up about Atlanta and not mention it never again."

"All right," Lon said, and glanced over Landon's shoulder in time to see his wife skulking along the wall of the house toward the shed. There was displeasure on her face.

"Yessir, I been working hard. Want a little tot of 'er?" Landon asked, pulling an old pint bottle from his hip pocket. He held it up and shook it. The bubbles rose and held. The liquor glistened through the clean, delicate glass of the old bottle, and the way that it glistened marked it as good liquor.

"That shore does shine good," Lon said. "Where did you get that old bat-wing bottle? I ain't seen one in I don't know when."

He knew that she was working her way in closer to them.

Landon waved the bottle about. "Don't worry about this old man," he said. "I've got plenty of bottles left over from the old days. I got bat-wings and some spider-web bottles and I've got a few *Old Maud* wine bottles left, I'll have you know."

Lon rose from his seat to look at the bottle, and to greet her.

"God a'mighty," he said; then she was with them.

"How are you, Landon?" she asked with the utmost courtesy, although the anxiety on her face was slowly transforming into anger, showing that she again felt the threat of liquor in her home.

Landon turned slowly to look at her, his shiny eyes wary, crafty. "Howdy," he said, and held out the bottle to her. "Would ye like a little snort yerself?"

She looked at each of them slowly. "Landon," she said, "I want to say something without hurting yore feelings. I'd like to have that bat-wing bottle when you finish with it. I'd pay you fer it. But I don't want the whisky and I don't want you tryin' to give Lon any."

Lon leaped up angrily. "By God, now, ol' woman. I thought I'd broke you a long time ago from deciding any sich things fer me."

He was trembling, biting his lips and batting his eyes rapidly.

She backed off, looking sorrowful. "Well, I'm sorry, then," she said, but she had had her say and it was not lost on Landon, despite his drunkenness. He stared at her, then handed the full bat-wing to her.

"Here, you can pour the brandy out and keep the bottle and do whatever you want with it," Landon said.

She stared at it, raked a finger slowly down her cheek, then took the bottle.

Lon took off his hat and beat his thigh with it angrily.

"Goddam," he said. "Goddam, Landon. Talk about giving the fox yer chicken to keep. Goddam."

She looked at him. "Shut yore mouth. I've got something else to say and you two birds jist listen. Landon, we're a-fixin' to sell three acres to a Floridy man an' . . ."

"You are? Where?" he demanded.

"Well, to tell the truth, it runs along your line," she said.

"Ga-odd damn," Landon gasped, pulling at his overall bib.

"Ga-odd damn," Lon echoed, whirling all about. "Why did you have to mention that right now?"

"Do you know what them sons-of-bitches do?" Landon asked, then answered, "They bring in bull dozers and rip up the land all over creation. They fill the streams up with mud and shit and ever'thing else and jist stay here a month or two a year. Why, that creek in yore lower pasture, and in both my fields, will run red mud fer a hundred years."

"Well, Lon is going to town with me day after tomorrow, and we're going to sign the deeds and they can have it."

"What? What?" Landon shouted. "Shit, do you need money? I didn't know you needed money. Let me buy it. I'll buy it. I'll buy yore whole goddam place. How much do you want fer it?"

Big Blue wandered up, sat, looked from under disconsolate hound brows at the antics of his master. The wind rose and blew some loose snowflakes about. Landon went to his dog and put his hand on top of his head.

"Big Blue," he declaimed dramatically. "Yes, all they is left to me is Big Blue. One time I had barns full of stock, a wife, a pack of good dogs, good crops . . ." He paused to stare at Lon and his wife. ". . . and two good neighbors, so I thought, anyway, to help me out. But many years ago my poor wife Berthy died, I sold the stock, the crops quit growing, and in the bitter end all they is left is a poor old drunk man with one good hunting dog because . . ." He turned and waved drunkenly at them. ". . . the good neighbors turned out not so good after all, because they're a-goin' to sell some land to the goddam outlanders, and if they build a house up here I'll personally burn the fucking thing down . . ."

Lon was slow to answer, but there was dark anger and determination in his eyes. "Now jist a minute, jist a minute, by God, Landon," he said, shaking his gnarled, farmer's finger at the other man. "You can stand here and cuss all day and I ain't got nothin' to say because me and her both uses sich as that in our talk, but you are not going to be blackguarding or vulgar in front of her, and by the great God, I mean that."

Landon had sobered a bit, nodded, and looked away. "I didn't mean to. I know better than that, Lon, I did not mean to . . ."

"Now I know that Big Blue is one helluva bear dog. I have been with you when he tangled with the meanest bear they wuz to be hunted. He is yore friend and he is my friend . . ."

Lon was getting underway with a drawn-out speech leading to some obscure point when she interrupted in cold anger. "Landon, take Big Blue and go back up that road and don't you come back down until you can git straight. Now we don't need the money, but them Floridy people think it's a pretty place fer a house and they was nice. They're a little pushy, but somehow they talked me into it and we're a-goin' to let 'em have it. You git Big Blue and go up that road, and I mean right now," she said.

Even with her anger and his state of intoxication, it was not lost on Landon that she did not offer to return the bat-wing. He muttered, pulled the dog's collar, and staggered up the old roadbed. He turned once and looked back, saw that they watched him.

"They's been people killed around here fer a lot less'n that." He swore darkly.

Then she went into the house, Lon with her. Both were trembling more from anger than from the chill. She set the full bat-wing on the warmer of her stove, stepped back and looked at it. She pulled her glasses tight around her ears and scrutinized the workings on the old glass closely.

"Yes, I bet 'tis good. And in such good glass," she said with a sensuality and desire he had not heard in her voice for years. He pretended not to notice; instead, he fixed his gaze on the snow glazing the pastures up the slope on Landon's place. He opened the window, let in the air, and checked it on the skin on his face and neck and the back of his hand.

"More snow in two or three days," he said. The air was sharp and clean, and even then the wind was coming in short rushes. She did not move for a while, then she happily began to sift some flour. He knew it was the presence of the liquor. It did that to some people. They did not have to drink any of it. All they needed was to know that it was nearby. It sang its own silent, sweet song to them. He noticed as the day wore on that the pretty, flat bottle remained where she had put it. He went out once to sharpen his axe, and when he returned, took notice that she had made no effort to pour out the liquor. Later he went to the barn to put hay in the horse's stall, and when he returned, the liquor remained untouched. He studied her unbeknownst. She was doing an open mating-dance around the kitchen, only it was directed toward the bottle.

He sat down in the straight chair and leaned it against the wall. In late afternoon, as she put the vittles on the table, he finally felt he could speak to her.

"Boy! Ol' Landon shore did git tore up when we mentioned about the land goin' to the flatlanders."

She stopped traipsing from the stove to the table, looked at her husband as if he were a stranger.

"Yes, well, it makes no difference. We're a-goin' to let them nice people have it. That's all there is to say about it," she snapped, then pulled her head back and fixed him with a defiant stare.

He shrugged, looked at the bottle. Yes, a wicked spirit in there. He felt vague stirrings in his gonads. Ah! He ate heartily, tried to get near her. No, he smelled no alcohol on her breath; she had not touched it.

That night in bed he rolled to her, pushing the hardness against her. She put her hands on his shoulders and pushed him away.

"No, we're too old. I'm thinkin' about somethin' else," she said.

He slid uncomplaining to his side of the bed, his feelings hurt for only a moment. Old? Yes, he was old enough to know that generally if you want something, all you have to do is wait for it. What is said today is not what is meant on another day. All things change. For the first time in many years a bat-wing sat in their house. That in itself was a sign of mighty change. Even then, as he was going to sleep, he heard the gusts of cold wind shaking the house. The next morning he again felt on those areas of skin, which he relied on for weather predictions, the promise of snow—maybe a big one. He grinned, smothered it. A big snow, huh? Cozy, cozy. Everything was in—plenty of wood, plenty of food.

She got up, padded in stocking feet to the stove without looking at the bottle, but he knew her very spirit was alive and aware of it. She wheeled around once and caught him looking at her, blushed, began fussing at him.

"I thought you said it was going to snow. Look out there. As clear as a bell and as windy as hell. It'll be a month before we see a cloud. That's how much you know."

"I don't have to know nothin'," he said. "Ol' woman, keep on and you'll git what you've been askin' fer. The snow don't care whether or not I know it's a-comin'. It wouldn't come jist to spite you, and it wouldn't not come jist to spite me. It comes when it will. I believe I'll jist take a little smell of that liquor that Landon meant to pour out."

"You keep your hands off that bottle," she commanded. "You'll get to drinkin' and be drunk as a cooter when them Floridy people meet us in the lawyer's office tomorrow to sign the deed. I don't think you ought to git near it."

"Oh, you had me all wrong, little darlin'," Lon said and pulled his lower jaw down in feigned surrender. "All I was goin' to do was jist pour it out. All you want is the bottle, an' . . ."

"Jist stay where you are, Mr. Lon. You jist stay where you are. I want it to sit there awhile. I might want to make a little camphor later on."

"Ah! I see. Well, let me know if you need any other ingredients, will you. Be sure that you do," he said. His smirk went unseen.

At supper that night he could see that she was growing more removed from their daily life. They bickered, but without energy, because her mind was somewhere else and he was too busy watching her, and trying to act like he wasn't watching her. They sat by the fireplace a bit later than usual—she crocheting and he listening to the hum and hiss of the burning wood—and talked about meeting the flatlanders to sign the deed. He noticed that the bat-wing had been moved to the fireplace mantel. As they went to bed, the bickering resumed, and whatever closeness they had managed at the fireplace vanished. She was remote, saying only the things that were needed to keep him at a distance. He kept to his side of the bed, now smiling in the dark, a hunter with the track of the quarry in sight.

At daylight she was vehemently against everything. The wood was not cut right, the mix in her woodbox was wrong. The flour that had sufficed yesterday was now faulty in every way. The fatback began to burn and smoke up the kitchen. He knew that she had burned it deliberately so that her anger could increase. She hurled a stick of stovewood at the wall, then threw away her batter and began to mix again.

He sat in the chair against the wall, not looking at her, his right eyelid drooping speculatively. The bat-wing was back on the stove warmer.

"Raise hell, you won't work." He repeated the old Appalachian saying, meant as an insult. He knew that she would ignore it.

After breakfast she became nervous and jittery. She began popping questions at him, even asking his advice: What should they wear to the lawyer's office? Should they hold out for more money? Did he really think a big snow was coming? And finally, tossed off carelessly: How much liquor and brandy did he reckon Landon had made? Lon grunted out answers, taking care not to smile or nod. Just a dumb old man.

They began dressing at eleven o'clock for the trip into town. He shaved carefully with the old straight razor, noticing that his hand was trembling. Sometimes his body told him more about the future than his mind was able to predict. There was some change coming. Was he apprehensive about selling part of his land? He went over the arguments again in his head, but decided to abide by the decision. She dressed with the bat-wing in the room with her so she could see it.

He was ready and standing by the window, thinking, when he realized that he felt some kind of anticipation—and was glad of it. Suddenly he saw Landon stagger around the last bend in the old roadbed. Landon was filling the whole road, zigzagging from one side to the other.

"Goddam," Lon muttered. "Drunker'n hell." He let out a low whistle. She entered the room behind him.

"What?" she asked.

"Here comes Landon."

"Well, what?"

"The whole road can't hold 'im."

"My Lord. My Lord a'mercy," she said. He noticed that she had toned down her language. But his nose detected nothing. She was guilty of something—or was she just planning to be guilty of something?

They drew back from the window a few feet so that Landon couldn't see them. He came on until he got to the edge of their yard, where he fell, raised himself, and sat. His face was red and morose. At last he rose unsteadily and came to the door.

His knock was feeble, uncertain. Lon answered, his face impassive so that his very lack of hospitality was filled with threat. She stood slightly behind her husband, her face a frozen mask. Landon stared from one to the other, rocking slightly in his brogans.

"Well, I want to know," he said, "is a man welcome here or not?"

"What do you want, Landon?" Lon asked coldly.

"Well, the first thing I want is to come in, if you don't mind, that is. It's a little chilly out here."

"Is what you have to say going to be long and drawn out?"

"By God, I jist want to ask a favor. I wouldn't be here a-tall if I didn't need a favor," he rasped.

They waited, knowing that this was part of an overture for making up, but uncertain as to whether or not they wanted to heal the breach.

Lon opened the door wider but so imperiously that it was not lost on Landon that they were extending only the normal hospitality given any man or beast in the perilous mountains.

Landon stomped in.

Finally he glared fiercely at them, and they at him.

"What?" asked Lon sharply.

"I need you to help me dig a grave," Landon said, his lip trembling slightly.

"What?" they said together. "Whose grave?"

He began to break. "Big Blue. He died last night," Landon said over a sob. "The pore thing. He died by hisself out beside the chimbley."

His grief was deep, heavy. They looked at each other a moment, at a loss. Finally Lon spoke in a voice devoid of sympathy or any other sentiment.

"Well, what the hell do you want me to do about it?"

Landon's eyes were full of spite. "Well, since I've begged fer this much out of you, I might jist as well beg you to show a little feeling fer a man who has lost the very last friend he had on this earth."

Lon was unmoved. "Well, I don't know what to do."

"You can help me dig a grave fer him. That's what you can do."

"Well, I'll be glad to give you a lesson in grave-diggin', but that's all the time I've got. We have to go sign the deeds. Now what you do is dig a hole in the ground deep enough fer old Big Blue, then roll him into it, put whatever dirt you dug out of the hole on top of him, pat it down a little, and that's all there is to it. I guess I've seen close to two thousand buryin's— man and beast—and that's the way they've done it ever goddam time. Good God a'mighty damn, I have never heard . . ."

"Here! Here! Here!" Landon said, and his voice reached for dignity. "You stop talking to me like that. It's Big Blue that's dead. You yerself have follered along after him and pulled him off more'n one bear. Who do you think you're throwing off on? Not jist some ordinary possum dog, no, Big Blue hisself, goddam it, and I'll thank you to tone it down."

He stopped, pulled a pint from his pocket, extended it in a brief offering. Then, without asking whether he might have a drink in their home, he took a good one. She watched him closely.

"God a'mighty!" he said breathlessly, "give me a drink of water."

Lon saw that she rushed to fill a glass. While she handed it to Landon, her eyes lingered on the bottle in his hand.

"I hate to bury him all by myself. He was all I had on this earth. I thought since you used to be my friend, and old Big Blue—he never done nothin' ag'in you, did he?—well, I thought you might give me a hand. I been drunk for a while and I guess I'll jist die drunk, but I ain't able to dig and besides I wanted somebody else there . . ."

"I never did see the beat of this. He wants me to officiate at a dog's funeral and I've got to go sign deeds for them goddam flatlanders. There's more trouble on any one day than mankind or the general public stops to realize. I have to go to that slick lawyer's office and . . ."

Landon stood, blinked, looked pitiable in his muddy overalls.

Then she reached out and touched her husband's arm.

"Go on up there," she said. "We've got plenty of time. If we're a few minutes late, they'll wait. He's been our neighbor fer a long time. Go up there. It won't take long."

"What?" he said and drew back.

"You go," she said.

Lon stood for a time, weighing it all. He walked about the house as if in deep thought—finally found the bat-wing on a table in the bedroom. Then he returned.

"Come on," he said to Landon.

"Stay till you git it done," she said.

The two of them climbed through the crusted patches of snow along the old roadbed, slipping here and there. Landon tried to make conversation a time or two, but he was not so drunk that he couldn't see Lon did not want anything said to him. When they arrived at Landon's place, Lon saw Big Blue, stiff, beside the chimney. He walked up to the body with an abrupt manner and said, "Bring me a goddam shovel and I'll git at it."

"No, no," Landon said, "he has to be laid in the cemetery. He is, and has been, one of the family."

"What? We have to walk up there?" Lon asked.

"Well, don't worry your head. I'll carry him."

"Yeh, an' I'll have to carry the shovel and mattock, won't I?"

Landon went to the barn for the tools and a pair of big feed sacks. He took a snort of liquor, hitched up his overalls, then picked up his dead bear dog. The two of them made their way through cold mud and snow crusts to the family cemetery, where Bertha and Landon's daddy and his daddy's daddy and numerous other relatives were buried. It was not unheard of for a good dog to be buried close to the family plot, but Landon picked out a place at the foot of his dead wife's grave.

"Here, dig it here," he said, and began sliding Big Blue into the sacks. Lon tested the frozen earth with the shovel and decided he had better break into the crust with the mattock.

"I know you want it here right now, but do you think you'll want it here later on?" he asked without emotion, watched Landon take a drink, then muttered, "I guess you will."

Lon took careful eye-measure of Big Blue and outlined a pit. Then he began to dig. From the cemetery he could see through a stand of spruce down to where the road from the highway came in to his own place.

"Listen Lon, do you reckon I ought to order one of them granite stone crosses for ol' Big Blue?"

Lon stopped digging, let his right eyelid droop. He took several long breaths. Finally he said, "I don't know, Landon. I shore don't know. Was ol' Big Blue a Christian?"

Landon's face saddened. "No, I don't believe he was, at that. I was jist allus a-goin' to git Berthy a cross and wound up with one of them double Georgia granites with room for both our names on it. That's all."

He turned and walked away. Lon returned to his digging, now in haste. He must leave soon. When he raised his head, he saw Landon wrapping the ensacked dog in a new, blue mackinaw, which increased the bulk considerably.

"Goddam! What are you up to?"

"I want him to be warm. I let him lay out there beside that chimbley and die in the cold, and now I want him to be warm and there ain't nothing wrong with that."

"I'll be goddammed, Landon. You shore are drunk, ain'che?" Lon said, looking back and forth from the dog to the grave.

"Naw, naw, it ain't that so much. I'm jist a lonely ol' man and my dog's dead, you son-of-a-bitch," he said testily. Nobody put "son-of-a-bitch" on a man without raising the possibility of murder—and they both knew it. "It's hell when the last thing you've got is gone, and got gone on a drunk when you're too old to git on a drunk. You've still got your wife, even your young'uns the hell and gone somewheres, but I never had any young'un except Johnny, an' the goddam Germans killed him."

He wheeled about and stumped off down the trail. Lon

resumed the digging. When he finished, he straightened up and saw Landon returning with a large bundle. Just as Landon reached the burying ground, Lon heard a car down in the cove and saw the flatlanders' blue Buick driving toward his house. He looked at his watch. He had not meant to spend so much time on the dog's grave. He turned around and glared at Landon, who had unrolled a thick 12' x 12' tarpaulin. Then Landon dragged the dog's body, already wrapped in the sacks and the coat, into the center of the tarp and slowly began enfolding it.

The dog's bulk, again increased, was now too large for the grave. Lon's face grew red, and he threw down the shovel. Suddenly he heard voices coming up the slope from his place. He thought he heard her curse.

"What?" he muttered to himself and turned his attention in that direction. Time passed slowly. Interminably. Then he heard her voice, loud and angry, and this was followed in quick succession by three shotgun blasts and some glass breaking.

"Aha!" he chortled. "The quail loads. I had three loads in that gun. They was too pushy fer her. I knowed it. I knowed it."

He heard the desperate spin of the flatlanders' tires in soft black mud, then heard the tires catch, and soon he saw the Buick careening up the little road. Lon stood for a long time, carefully weighing all he had learned. Landon waited, his eyes tracing a confused path between the burying ground and the cove below.

"C'mere a minute, Landon," Lon said softly.

"What?" he asked warily.

"Gimme a drink of that goddam liquor," Lon said. Landon reached into his overalls and handed over the bottle. There was a bit less than half a pint. Lon drank it down, gasped, wheeled about, whistled, then got himself together.

"Them is good herbs, right enough, Landon. Go down to your place and set me two jars out, you hear me?"

Landon nodded. "Oh Lord," he muttered. "He's gonna git on one."

Lon grinned. All traps had been sprung, and no guilt tainted him. He had merely watched and waited. Thick clouds had come in quickly, and big flakes of snow fell slowly down.

"Listen, Landon," he said warmly, "you jist tell me how much more clothes you're a-goin' to put on Big Blue so I'll know how deep to dig this here grave."

The
Moon
Bather

S HE LIVED IN THE SMALLEST OF THE THREE
summer villages, but because no one else conjured, she had
to travel occasionally to the other camps. The small camp was
the most important because the chiefs worked out of it, and
the chiefs worked out of it because it was the smallest and the
river was wider and quieter there and canoes could come and
go and the affairs of the tribe could best be handled there. The
camp was made up mostly of adults, although a few children
were allowed to stay there. There was another village several
miles upstream for the warriors and hunters and their families.
The third camp, the largest one, was hidden in a cove away
from the big waters.

Her name was Sore Paws. She sat at her work with the dye
pots, between her lodging and the river, and watched the river.
There had been much coming and going in the past few weeks
while the chiefs and council tried to decide whether to close
this camp. There was big trouble in the other villages, but as
yet no one had died here. And so the important men came and
went.

The bright sun drew down into the autumn afternoon. She
looked up from her work and saw a canoe coming upstream,
cutting back and forth in the current. As it headed straight
toward her place, she felt the skin and hair along the back of
her neck lift slightly. The man in the canoe sat straight and
handled the paddle well. When he was still a hundred feet out,
she felt his eyes upon her, unwavering. She stared back at him

as he jammed the bow of the canoe into the sandy bank near
her pots.

Sore Paws walked to the canoe and saw that he traveled with
little. There was a rolled-up bobcat skin, which might hold
food because flies were around it. There was a short bow, a
club, a short blowgun, and six darts. She also noticed a good
robe made of several wolf skins stitched together. Other people
of the village, mostly women, stared at the stranger. Most of
the men had gone into the forest for the big deer hunt and
would be gone for days.

He pulled his things from the canoe and smiled at her.
Unbidden, he walked to her fire and stared into her big pot.
Though his markings were not of her tribe, he was one of the
mountain people and spoke her tongue.

"Is it all right if I stay at your place awhile?"

She nodded.

"For how long?" he asked.

"We will think about it. It all depends on whether you are
a disappointment or not. It is strange that in this moon the only
visitors on the river have come downstream, and yet you have
come up. I want to ask you about that."

He looked at the river, nodded tiredly. "There has been a
strange thing about movement on the river, if you have
noticed."

"Yes, my nose is not useless, as some are," she said.

"There," he said, pointing out across the water. "There are
two more dugouts full of women and children. They are all
dead too."

They turned and made differing religious gestures in respect
for the passing dead, then stood silently and watched the big
poplar dugouts move out of sight down the river.

"I will tell you," he said. "Do you know the big falls downstream? I passed by there. It is a place of bad spirits and scaven-
gers now. The dead are everywhere, floating in the big pool
under the falls, and big fish are biting at them. The dead clog

the drainways, and broken canoes and dugouts litter the banks. The people are using canoes to flee from something that does not arrive in canoes."

He looked into her big pot and saw that she was soaking oak splits for a basket.

"You are making good dye. I would have brought yellow root."

"I have enough yellow root," she said. "I will cook food. What are you called?"

"Slow Tracker. What are you called?"

"Sore Paws. My hands were sore and cracked when I was learning my trade as a child. Are you called Slow Tracker because you stay steady on a track until you run it to the end?"

He shook his head deprecatingly, withstanding the shrewd feminine probing. He knew that she did not care about his tracking skills. She was testing his vanity.

The water in the small pot began to simmer. She spoke.

"Our chiefs are seeing many dead people on the river, and they talk about closing the river villages and spreading the people into the land until death passes. They think it has to do with the river, even though people on the land are dying, too. We are not many here, and nobody has died. But in our next village up the river there are dead, and they are burning their bodies in their huts instead of putting them on the water to float away."

She took down some jerked meat from a pole across the front of her lean-to. He took it from her hands.

"What is it?" he asked.

"Forgive me. It is only a bit of raccoon. I have to get by. I have no man. I make dyes and weave baskets and make pots and arrows, and sometimes I conjure and have visions. No one else here conjures. Now, about you. You are not marked or beaded like a warrior or a hunter. I cannot get you fixed. What do you do?"

"I have a calling. I go around and see into things. I find medi-

cines for people. Sometimes I see futures and sometimes I divine
the past which has made the present. What is happening now
is hard to say. I gathered herbs and sweated and then I had a
vision that people would be dying, so I started moving about,
and soon I found that it was so. I do not stay long in one place.
I was a warrior at one time, and a war chief, but that was in
other times."

"How old are you now?" she asked.

He hesitated, a mocking light in his eyes.

"I have known fifty summers exactly as the last one ended.
I find it interesting that you are not with a man. How many
winters have burned your lonesome cheeks with wind?"

"Thirty-two. My cheeks do not stay lonesome always. I
have had my men, but I did not like them long."

He nodded. "Perhaps if someone spent enough time to find
out about you and show you."

She was thoughtful.

"Very well. If you know enough to say that, you may bring
in your robe and stay the night. Then we will see," she said.

He placed his belongings on her sleeping robes, then took his
pipe from his bundle and lit it. He sat near the fire. She put the
jerky in the hot water so it would grow soft.

"You need not do that," he said. "I thank you for the courtesy but I still have my teeth." He stared at her fiercely, then
bared his teeth.

"It will be easier on your stomach. It was a tough animal and
I boiled it some before I dried it but I found it needs more."

She brought some fresh nuts and a small assortment of roots.
They ate from the pot with their fingers. Then she poured
strong tea. Several of the village women stirred about, staring
at him, then returned to their own shelters. She cleaned the
pots and put them away, and they sat quietly as darkness fell.
Autumn chill flowed in with the river and they listened to the
muffled whispers of the water spirits.

He said, "It is bad to be on the river at night unless you are going to war. Especially this river. The spirits are hurt and angry. They might even come up out of the water."

"No. You do not understand these spirits. If you are saying that to bring me closer, you do not have to. Now, tell me about your time as a warrior. Did you count coup many times?"

"I had my day. I killed many but I always felt it was better to humiliate enemies and count coup without killing. It was such thinking that led me into the red visions, and then some of the old men said I was not meant to be a brave forever, or a chief. They said I was to turn toward that light in my heart and it would take me to the right places and to the right people all my life. I have been doing the visions a long time. There is something strange in me. I felt it move and turn over as I came up the river, and I came straight to you. Do you feel that you have something to tell me?"

"I may later on. I do not know. It is time we went inside," she said.

She lit a greasy wick in a gourd full of fat. It took him but a moment to remove his clothing. He stood lithe and mature and hard, dark-skinned in the flickering light. Her sleeping robes had a clean smell, with the faint hint of her own scent and a vaguely familiar odor which he finally recognized as the smell of the strong tea. She remained clothed, kneeling and looking at him for a time. It did not make him uncomfortable or uneasy. He sensed in her a spirit that dealt with time as he did, so he did not question her rituals.

Abruptly she stood and in one quick movement disrobed. He moaned at the beauty of her complexion, which was of a deeper and darker hue than that of other women, but with a liquid luminosity, a shimmering of varied depths. Slowly she brought her burnished, ghostly body nearer to him, and it caught light as she moved and spun off silvery glints. He rose to her with a low, helpless roar in his throat. It was as if he had sought through many dark days and in desolate lands to find at last this woman who reflected some obscure part of himself.

And so they loved in an unreasonable and fierce manner until they no longer recognized or knew themselves as separate beings.

They emerged very slowly. He set up a deep, vibrating hum, which he held for minutes and which went out and into the village and onto the dark sliding waters, and then he ceased. Minutes passed and the two of them clutched each other by the shoulders.

"What was that call you made?" she asked.

"You turned into a snake of some kind that I did not recognize. I wanted to still and soothe it. Did that happen?"

"Yes. Where did you learn it?"

"From a place in my heart. I have always known it."

"Now what is it that you need to know about me?"

"Your skin. How do you get it like that?" he asked, looking at the gleams and the changeable lights flashing from her.

She laughed. "I sought a secret place on the mountain. Everyone has such a place, but you must find it for yourself and you know when it is the right one because you feel it. Nobody can find you there. At that place you must lie naked in the sun during the time that the moon is dark and during the time that it is waxing. When it rains you go to the place and lie naked against the earth, letting the rain flow over your body and dry away. You must also spend time there naked in the morning air and in the evening air and in the night air.

"But the most important thing is the moon bath. For the three nights before the full moon and for the three nights afterward, I go to stand in the moonlight and sing old low songs that I know, and it is then that I can feel something passing over me and going through my skin. I also bathe in the tea that I make, but mostly it is the moon and the feeling that I get. Perhaps the skin does not glisten as much except in the deeper light of you. Perhaps I am only a moon to the sun in you. You are a person of the sun and you can understand."

He clutched her tighter. "Does anyone else do this for you?"

"No one."

"And how did you learn about the moon?"

"Like you. It has always been in my heart. The wind made quiet suggestions and I knew of the moon and the sky. I have tried to make such a love as ours with a few warriors, but none had the true fire. Your fire is strong and it is banked and controlled."

They came together and breathed in unison and let their pulses join. Near dawn they slept.

The following day was spent at small tasks, but inwardly they were shaken and marveled at their loss of balance. In their minds they knew of channels between a man and a woman in which great powers could flow back and forth. The women of the village—the sensitives—were aware that a rare event had taken place between a man and a woman. They came to call, their excuses unclear, and stared curiously at him, his fringes and beading. He met their stares. All morning the woman and her man kept silent, but near noon they spoke together.

"My meeting with you has meaning," he said. "I am as dizzy as a child at the edge of a cliff. When I came up the river I was not sure why I came, for I could not receive a clear vision. Your chiefs will see another sun-up before they ask me to account for being here. Here I am with your lights bedazzling me. I think that I was sent for you to reveal to me what my direction is to be."

He looked silently into her chinquapin eyes and at her arms and neck and face. The lights did not move so quickly now, but they were visible and the power and strength of her seemed to be rising. She spoke.

"I will speak to the council. They will want to know if you are a Cherokee or a Creek or a Choctaw or what. Also they will notice that you are old enough to be sitting at council somewhere. What is the truth?"

He lit his pipe.

"Tell them my mother was a Cherokee and my father was a Creek. They also met beside a river. Soon after my birth a war party captured my father and they laid him close to a big fire to roast his eyes out, but my mother and her brother spoke for him. He had to renounce himself, over and over, for a long time. With that tribe he was killed in a battle at a place east of here in the flat country. I fought my battles as a Cherokee and was chief of several large war parties for some winters. I never wanted to be a chief, and when I was old enough to practice politics and join a council, I had already begun to conjure. I have no wife but I have had women. I have sired children. There was a time of planting in women's fields and farming. I was also a hunting chief for a time. But since I began to have visions I have traveled the land and I have seen many good things and a great many bad spirits. They are lurking about everywhere, as is known to you. Those evil ones sometimes make me fall sick for a while. I can see their souls rotting away like the flesh that rots on a corpse."

She looked at him sharply. "I see that I can learn much. But the council will want to know why you started to conjure so late. Most begin as boys."

"Tell them that I had clear dreams all my life. When a red haze came over my dreams, the old men said it was a definite sign for me to begin magic. Later the haze came over my waking visions. Since then, all has gone well."

She went about the village seeking out the leaders. When she returned, she began to build up a fire and did not speak. Slow Tracker went to the river and lined up stones in the shallow water. Wading into deeper water, he maneuvered several fish into the stone trap. He gutted them and wrapped them in leaves and mud and buried them in the coals. As they ate, her face lit up and his desire for her rose. He drank tea and stared into the bowl.

She said, "The fish are cooked in a way not known to me. They are good. Was it the leaves?"

"Yes, and the way that I covered them. What did the leaders say?"

"They are interested in what you are doing. They said to stay as long as you need to. Soon the hunters will be back with deer. If you want to stay that long, you can help with the meat and the tanning."

In the early evening they again came together by the light of the burning tallow. Each gave the fire of love to the other and fanned the flames. And to cease for a moment's rest brought the terrible pain of knowing that they filled each other's empty parts and that a time would come when the fullness must flow out again.

He stayed with her three days. Then he knew it was time for him to go up the river. He told her that after two passages of the sun he would leave the water and go into the mountains to other small villages he knew about. Then he would fast and sweat and stay awake until a clear idea rested in his head.

The feel of autumn was chill upon the land now, and though the afternoons held heat and flies, a bite was hidden in the air. She gathered his things for him and took them to the canoe. She had treated his robe with her dark tea, and now the aroma of her would go with him. They did not touch again. He sat back in the craft, paddle ready, and looked at her.

"You are my woman and you know that. I am your man and I know that. No matter where I go or what I do I will be thinking of you, so it would be a lie to say that I am not your man. I know now my dreams will be filled with you and the thought of you will strengthen my visions. I will return when I can. Do you feel that I have become your man in these nights?"

"Yes," she said. "I will be here."

Then he pushed free with the paddle and slid the canoe

across the water up the right side of the river in the quiet water, away from the curls of the current. Some of the women stood outside their houses and watched him pass.

Now and then he had to portage over or around rocks, logs, and sand bars because the river grew narrow and the current was too much to fight. But when he resumed paddling he let his mind go to the place of images and thoughts. This was the early stage of preparing himself for the full, fearsome power of the vision. And as he had predicted, the experience with the woman had increased his powers.

That night he slept close to the water, not afraid of bear or panther or hostile warrior. Two things were now in the air. One was the great lassitude and well-being that comes upon the earth as autumn sings its ancient harvest song. Animosities and hungers are few among the creatures at this time. The other thing was the death which had come so quietly and to so many. Men were not quick to harm each other when the earth itself was killing. He made his food, then lay down under his overturned boat. He chanted and prayed and went deeper into that darker spiritual ground from which he must extract an answer. He went from prayer into sleep, where more of the vision must form, and he saw briefly the fading remnant of the crop moon as it waned. For a moment he saw her and smiled. But he did not find even a hint of the answer.

The next day he went further up the river, but he quit the water at midday because it was getting narrow and fast. It was good water to ride with, but it was not profitable to buck the current. He found a well-hidden docking between two sloping rocks where a small creek joined the river. He tipped the canoe until it was full of water, then put enough small rocks inside to sink it. He tied his robe and other things with thongs, put his bow on his back, and hid the blowgun under a log. Then he climbed the steep ridge above the water. He did not rest, nor did he need to. He penetrated the forest quickly.

The forest in autumn. Its sharp evocations, its painful lost music raised the sharp edges of his magic. Something spoke briefly in his brain—he saw the flash of something white. Autumn. Leaves curing, turning, curling, drifting. It was as if he walked in a vast and fragrant tea loft. The thing white flashed in his mind, but it did not tarry long enough for him to decipher. Near night he made a low lean-to from spruce boughs and ate some of the jerked raccoon she had given him. He sought his vision, but it eluded him. The time was not right for it.

He walked for three days, finding a number of dead people in the forest. Mostly hunters, they had not died by violence, Then he found a small, temporary village with the death posts set up at the periphery. He walked in slowly, making signs to the spirits so they would know it was he who had no harm or malice in his soul. The death posts were a sign of mourning, and in addition, they warned that death was powerful here, so powerful that it not only took people but might also evaporate evil spirits.

Slow Tracker found that death was totally allied with the people here. A burial mound had been started and some bodies were covered, but their survivors had also been taken and were dead in the bark houses. Death had not surprised them, because all except three were in their sleeping robes. He counted forty-two bodies, including eight children. They had not starved, for several deer skins were drying, and he had seen the meat in every hut. He walked to the springs and smelled and tasted the water.

Then he went to the central fire, where the medicine bones and beads were hung. He flung cold ashes about, chanting for shadows to give up their secret forces and spirits. He shook his turtle shell rattle, then carried it and the snake rattles, shaking them here and there among the dead. Slowly a thin thread of intuition grew from deep inside his consciousness and stitched together parts of a vision. But still there was not enough. He squatted beside the main fire pit and ran his fingers through the powdered ash. It was late in the day when an urgent voice shouted to him from beyond the death posts. He saw a warrior waving to him. His trappings showed him to be a mountain tribesman. Slow Tracker went to him.

"Hiya! Hihihiya! Are you not afraid to go past the death posts?" the warrior asked.

"No. I have good spirits with me. You seem worried."

The warrior's cheeks were sad. They fell down the side of his face like a wet buzzard's wings.

"I need your medicine. I have eighteen with me, up on that ridge. Come and talk with us. Do you plan to sleep with the dead?"

"Yes, I will sleep here. Maybe there will be a struggle between death and the other spirits and I will watch the fight. If I have no fear, nothing will happen to me and my medicine will get stronger. But I will come with you for a time."

The brave wheeled and trotted away and Slow Tracker fell in behind him. In an hour they entered a big clearing on the side of a sweeping ridge. The other braves stood about the clearing, their spears, bows, mauls, and hammers leaned against the rocks. They were not surprised at a stranger's appearance. An older warrior arose from where he was seated and came forward.

"Hiya! Our man down there saw you walk into the death place. He said that you waved medicine and shouted back the spirits. By what authority? What are you doing here?"

"Tracking death."

"What?"

"I am Slow Tracker. My job is to go upon the land and to move upon the waters. I once was a warrior and a chief but I saw a different light. I mean no harm. I stay here and there. The people have begun to die off in large numbers and my heart said for me to go and see what spirit works at this. You seem to have a small war patrol here. Are you the chief?"

"I am now. We were three times this number when we got

into a battle one moon past. Many men were killed. Our enemy came out of the north. Perhaps they were from the six tribes joined together and wanted to capture slaves. Now these braves you see here are beaten and cowardly and I need them to fight. Our enemy follows us. I myself scouted them once and I know that we could beat them if these men would fight. No. They will not. They are nervous and frightened. We have been living on squirrels and fish for days. I want you to tell me how to breathe the fight back into them."

Slow Tracker looked around, saw that each had individual courage and will, suspected that each now distrusted the others and distrusted the group's ability to fight well. He said, "Build up a fire and let me see what I can."

The old warrior and another built a fire. Slow Tracker knelt before it, his thoughts swimming away like an otter. However, his eyes watched the embers fall in smoldering patterns—red and white and black—and his eyes kept his brain connected with present reality while a slow wave of darkness came and went out, taking with it his thoughts. Much later, his thoughts returned with clear knowledge. It was near dawn. The brave who was guarding him went to awaken the chief warrior.

"They are coming here," Slow Tracker said. "They will be here in four sun-ups."

The chief nodded, then said: "We can't run much further. Perhaps I ought to break them up and let them take a chance by themselves in the woods, but the big death is probably on our people by now. How can I get them to fight?"

Slow Tracker stared at the trees and into the sky. He felt the air.

"Use the sun. There is still some heat to it. For three days make them lie in the sun with no clothing or shade and very little water. Let the light and the heat get into their stomachs and heads."

"That is a torture. They will go crazy."

"Some may die," Slow Tracker said. "Have you never heard

of it? Warriors are the sun's people. You must give them no food for the first two days. Let them eat a little on the third. The sun brings more madness than the moon."

He thought of Sore Paws a moment, felt desolate. He continued.

"They cannot guess how brave they can be. Very mean and crazy. The sun will get into their blood like the venom from wasps. It will rot their fear as snake poison rots the flesh. You can trap your enemies in this clearing. Do not let even one of them get away."

Then he ate some roasted groundhog with them.

"Now I ask a favor," he said. "Tell me if you have circled widely across the land."

"Yes," the old fighter said.

"Is the death big?"

"Everywhere. I fear that no one will escape."

Slow Tracker returned to the small village. He fetched his robes and slept all afternoon near the death posts. That night he built a small fire and huddled near it, shaking the rattles, chanting softly, pulling the good spirits from the hidden places of his soul. He let his spirits out slowly on strong chains like grim hunting dogs to smell out lurking bad spirits. As he slipped into his trance, he felt the spirits go beyond his reach and control, doing their silent and invisible battles. Fear came unbidden to his face like a cloud of dangerous gnats. He chased it away time and again. But when daylight came he had learned nothing. Exhausted, he ate a small piece of the jerky, drank water, and slept. When he awakened, he began in earnest the fasting and sweating in preparation for the vision.

He emptied his bladder and stomach, then wrapped himself in his robes and sat some distance from the fire pit. The sun soon raised a sweat. From time to time he uttered doleful chants as the hours passed and darkness came. When the air chilled he wrapped more tightly in the robes so that the sweating would continue. Soon he realized that an important message awaited, because there was movement of old memories through his brain—but none from the dark land which gave visions. The harder it was to draw up a vision, the purer it would be when it came. Even as dawn came and passed into a bright blast of light he watched the stream of recollection—meals he had eaten, a child's drum, the fearful time before battle, the calmness of spirit once battle was joined, a bow made by his grandfather which had remained in the family until the old ones died in a winter storm and the unprotected heirlooms went into the hands of marauders, and on and on and on. Then the images stopped coming in sequence and exploded into his consciousness in one vast bulk . . .

By afternoon the chants arose in his throat of their own accord and his head swayed on his neck. Yet nothing new came. In the night he became giddy and was strongly tempted to stop straining after visions and return downriver to the woman. But he had been shaped by the discipline of many sweats and fasts, so he remained at it, his eyes locked forward, peering grimly toward an empty field across which must march the vision. Before dawn another set of low chants formed in him, then he began to moan and the moans joined together and became wails as dawn broke. It was then, in the first light, that he sent up his death song. It broke first from his chest like an asthmatic cough, then from his throat with a terrible vibrance and resonance that stirred the spirit world. Abruptly the cry ceased and his inner eye watched patiently, intently, as sensation dissolved into grayness without form or boundary. His thoughts became a stream that overflowed into the low places until they filled, then flowed on.

A bounding flash of white.

Then he saw the war patrol, and they were all dead but the old one. He saw nothing of the enemy.

White! It whirled at the edge of his mind, taunted, disappeared. Death in the villages. The people were fallen everywhere. He saw the run of water in the river above the village where she was. It came, white, toward him. Panther? Tlonttu tsi? Eagle? No. It was on the ground. Skilly? Ghost?

He saw her face. It wrenched a cry from him. She was serious, warning him. The white streak came. He felt no threat. Then looking into flat whiteness, he saw a blood map. Rivers and forks and deltas of redness.

Then the images ceased. He trembled, trying to come about gradually. The images must slowly settle into their secret bins. Much later he began slowly stretching his limbs. He ate some of the jerky and drank water. Then he relieved himself.

He walked about, deep in study, trying to decipher the signals of his vision. He slept and dreamed of a white deer, awakened and nodded to himself. Then he gathered his robes, weapons, and rattles. He was about to decamp when the yelps of a battle on the ridge came to him. Later he heard warriors coming and hid himself in one of the huts to watch. Some of the northern war party passed, in flight—bloody, in rout. He waited until the next day and warily made his way toward the clearing on the ridge. He was puzzled, for the old warrior met him with a mighty howl of glee.

"Come. Come. You are a good man. As you can see, we beat them off. We only lost three braves."

The corpses of the enemy were strewn about where they had fallen in the ambush.

"My braves fought well. They were crazy with the fires of the sun. They said they were weakened, but when the time came they caught on fire. I am their leader, yet I was afraid of them they were so mean. I have not heard such snarling and howling before."

Slow Tracker nodded, guardedly. He had seen these same braves in the vision, but they were dead. If one part of the vision was wrong, perhaps all of it was.

"Have something to eat," the old warrior said. "We killed two deer at dawn. What a good sign. It is time we had good food. Some of our men are gathering acorns for bread. Here, magic man, have meat."

"No. I have fasted and it would hurt my stomach. I must go farther into the mountains. I had my vision, but I do not yet understand, so I will travel. But I will return to this place."

With that he arose and walked past the warriors, and they raised their weapons to him. He went past the spine of the ridge to the other side and found a game trail to follow. He came upon numerous deer and found it strange that they did not bound away. He concluded that, because he was not carrying harm in his heart, he did not glow with the threatening spirit that would frighten them.

He still trembled from weakness, but he ate the jerky and now his stomach could appreciate the fact that she had boiled it before it was dried. For two passages of the sun he went on, then decided he was moving away from the answer rather than toward it, so he turned in his tracks. The winds were now sharp and chill, and at night he wrapped tightly in his robes. Leaves sailed down with each breeze, and the fragrance of the forest intensified. When he reached the clearing where the battle had been fought, he saw the truth of his vision. There was no sign of violence on the dead warriors, so he knew the big death had touched them. He hurried to the chief, who lay beside a rock.

"Do you know what it was?" he asked the chief.

"No. I try to think but I cannot. I am very sick. I have seen my own death coming. A while ago it came to the edge of the clearing and looked at me."

"What did it look like?"

"Just death. I did not look at it long. It looked at me for a long time."

"You must think. What was it that you and all your men did in common?"

"I have tried. Nothing. All of the people are going to die. I am not afraid to die. But I am afraid when everyone has to die. The spirits and animals will take over the earth. The people are guilty of bad hearts. It is not any one person or village. Many people lie. Others steal and kill. Now extinction is coming. Not one will escape this."

"Be quiet. It is my job to talk and predict and explain," said Slow Tracker.

But the old warrior's eyes looked at the edge of the clearing and began to cloud over. He gave his death chant and smiled; then he was gone.

Slow Tracker arose, looked about for a moment, saw nothing significant. Then he went down the wooded slope to the little village. No curious person had intruded there. The winds blew past the posts and among the huts. He looked about, shaking his head. He fell to his knees, held out his hands to implore. Then he saw a flash of white among the trees nearby. He picked up his bow and two arrows. White flashed again. He walked to the edge of the village. He was weary but unafraid. Then he saw coming toward him a sacred white deer. It came within a few yards of him and stopped. Though he did not will himself to do it, he raised the bow and shot an arrow into the white deer's side. It did not leap and run as was usual with such a wound. Rather it fell suddenly, dead, unmoving. He carried it into the village and hung it from one of the meat-dressing tripods near the fire holes. Ringing its ankles with his knife, he quickly stripped off the skin and threw it over one of the poles. He gutted and dressed out the carcass. As soon as he had made a fire, he ran a spit through the chunk of meat and roasted it. After eating his fill, he rested awhile, then went to the skin in order to put ashes on the wet hide. It was then that he noticed the blood-maps on the inside of the skin—rivers and islands, forks and deltas. No blood was near the arrow wound, itself an insignificant slit, so the maps were not caused by hemorrhaging. Still he did not comprehend.

When he awakened the next morning he was sick in his

stomach and his eyes were grim. Slowly he got his things together and lurched through the forest to the cascading river. He found his canoe, but realized he must rest before attempting to bring it to the surface. He slept until dawn. Then he took off his clothing, slipped into the cold water, removed the stones, and surfaced the canoe. He pushed it far enough onto the bank to dump the water and found that the bark and pitch still held. He began to tremble and rested for a while. Then he loaded his things and pushed the craft into the current. He lay back on his bundle as the thread of the stream caught him and shot the canoe down narrow gorges and foamy slides.

He weakened steadily. He feared that the fasting and sweating had thrown him off balance. The canoe shot ahead, and at one rough run of water, it switched direction and was suddenly becalmed in a placid backwater. He looked down into the water and saw the wreckage of two canoes and several bodies suspended in the pool, halfway to the bottom. Slow Tracker stood, his legs jerking, but he managed to spread his robes in the canoe. He took out his rattles and a thong of rawhide with which he tied the ritual knots.

"Death will take me and I know it," he said aloud. "My death has found my trail and it has followed me and it is coming fast. I cannot elude it."

He shook his rattles and chanted low in his throat. The canoe drifted into an underwater tangle of roots and limbs and held. He looked at the roots for a moment without comprehension, then fell back unconscious.

At midday he came dimly awake. Though he was now prepared for death, he felt his spirit tell him to move on, down the river. He freed the craft of its entanglement and pushed it into the tailing swirls of the rapid water. Again he was hurled through narrow gorges and brushy ravines. He soon lost consciousness, and it was not until after dark that he roused again. The river was gentler, wider. The full moon had topped the trees in the east and glistened on the water. About him, in the water, were several dead bodies drifting with the flow. His canoe cut the soft, slow water. He tried once to raise his paddle, then lay back, too weary. He knew where he was. He watched the left bank of the river as it passed his canoe. A mile before he reached the village he knew it had been bad. The odor of burnt wood was in the air, and he guessed that as they had died off the survivors had burned the shelters.

The moon swelled in the sky as his canoe came around the last turn. It appeared that the entire village had burned. His head was unsteady as he raised up to see more. At the far end of the clearing he saw her place and saw a wisp of smoke rising from her fire pit. He rose to his knees and stared.

Yes, her. Glistening in the moonlight like a great otter afire with stars and comets. She walked slowly toward the river. He reached for his paddle, then felt his mind falling away. Later he felt the boat drifting and could not open his eyes. He listened, heard the wolves along the ridges. At last he made his eyes open. She was tucking his robes about him. She went to the bow of the canoe and knelt. She was wet and nude, beautiful and luminous in the chill moonlight. He sweated, his head shook. He could not see her face clearly. She held out a gourd cup with a long neck. He recognized the strong tea.

"I knew you were on the river because my arm started to glow awhile ago," she said.

He sucked from the neck of the jug.

"The deer are all sick," he said. "They are not dying but the people are eating the deer and the people are dying. I ate some of it..." His hand found the uncured fur of the white deer and held it out.

"It is on there," he said. "The disease is marked by the blood maps."

"I know," she said. "Our hunters came back and we feasted. Then they all died. I have been making tea and drinking it and praying. Maybe it will save us."

Again he fell away from the earth and into the sky. It seemed for a moment that he floated above the canoe and saw the lights rising from her in great excitement. Time passed in a flare of light everywhere. Sweat poured from him as he awakened, giddy. He felt pleased with them both, together.

He watched her. The lights gleamed in her depths. He reached out to feel whether the lights held heat, but he fell back in convulsions. Now the lights passed up into her face and he saw great peace there. She sat at the front of the canoe and stared at him and past him. A swollen full moon shone over her left shoulder. His hand fell and trailed in the water. He heard the pack of wolves howling on a far ridge. The current quickened and the roar of the big falls sounded in the distance.

Sam Welch
Is Not
The Name
of a
White
Man

IT IS PASSING STRANGE, BUT I HAVE NEVER heard one of those boys who was up in the cliffs that morning mention it. I think it is time to tell it, but I will have a hard time getting it all in one piece because when I got to recollecting, I remembered all the other things too. I don't know why I decided to tell about it now. Maybe I am getting old and loose in the tongue, or maybe it's like Sam said, that the day comes for everything. It was better than thirty years ago. Maybe the day has come.

But do not think I am too old, now. I just act old sometimes to get out of working, or fighting. Sometimes I act deaf if I don't want to be hearing some things. Generally words just cause trouble—I learned that from Sam, too. But I can hear a good fish jump in the creek, and I can hear a buck soft-toeing around in the laurel. Going Home Redhorse claims I can hear the top on a can of Budweiser snap a mile away.

Going Home also didn't like the deputy with funny eyes who used to wait on the bridge for us when we went into Bryson City. But Going Home has always been easygoing and scared of deputies. When he got in town drinking and they caught him, he always went along, playing like a good drunk Indian, never giving anybody trouble, and he got away with it.

Going Home has an easy job now. He ordered a big Sioux war bonnet from somewhere in North Dakota and a buckskin outfit from someplace in California. When the tourists come in the late spring, he goes and stands in front of the Boundary Tree Restaurant and Motel, looking grim, and charges tourists a quarter to pose for their pictures. He calls himself Chief Red Hawk and shakes hands with the people and holds their children—or sometimes dogs—while they make pictures. He also charges them for signing his name in some symbols that he made up. He can write as good as anybody, but he don't want the tourists to know it. We went to school together, and after the war we went to college over at Cullowhee, and later, even taught school. But not many Indians and no white men at all know about that now. Going Home also does the happy buffalo dance for the tourists, once in a while, when he's been drinking. He tries to get money out of them for dancing, but he don't do as well as old man Jeff Sullins over on the other side of Soco Gap in Haywood County.

Jeff grew a beard and got a big black hat and tries to look like what the flatlanders think a mountaineer ought to look like. He picks his banjo in a filling station parking lot and sometimes the tourists throw coins to him. He said he cleared more than $300 one week. Then they put in that Mile-High Ghost Town on the mountain above Maggie Valley, and the cowboys and gunfight and chairlifts about took all the tourists' attention and money from old Jeff. So he asked Going Home to team up with him. Him and Going Home might have worked up something there except in a couple of days they got to drinking, and Jeff got mad or crazy and maintained there was no such thing as a happy buffalo dance. Then Going Home said that Jeff could only pick one tune on the banjo and that was "Bill Bailey"—and he played that rather poorly. Jeff hit Going Home over the head with his banjo and broke three of the big, painted turkey feathers on that Sioux bonnet. Going Home jerked out his knife and cut a place on Jeff's thumb, then kicked his banjo off the rock wall and into the creek. That's not been but a couple of years ago.

Going Home's last name sounds Indian, but in the old Cherokee it would be Red Horse. Redhorse is the white man's name for a trash fish. Somehow or other it got mixed up on the tribal rolls about four generations ago and it came down to Going Home as Redhorse.

Going Home's happy buffalo dance is how everybody first got to know about the crazy mean deputy that they swore in over at Bryson City. He wasn't a regular deputy, just one of those special deputies that are supposed to be at the beck and call of the sheriff and serve at his pleasure. But for some reason this one, by the name of Bill, wore his badge all the time, kept his pistol in sight, and waited around the bridge that crosses the river before you get to Bryson City. He was always there on Friday and Saturday and Sunday to jump on all the Indians going to town. Any Indian, old woman, young boy, married woman—it didn't matter to him—he liked to say smart things to them and make threats. Everybody called him "Spreading Adder" for a while, since he seemed to be like the snake that puffs up and hisses but won't bite.

Anyway, it is a long road from the village to the bridge, and Going Home had stopped off at a couple of places and had some drinks. He took one last drink at a white man's house right before you get to the bridge, and when he reached it, he did the happy buffalo steps all the way across. Going Home didn't know who the deputy was. He said that he noticed the man wore a gun on his belt, but then, most white men from the mountains had guns. Anyway, Bill stopped Going Home at the far end of the bridge and showed him his badge, then beat the shit out of him and took him to jail for thirty days.

Bill's funny eyes were set close together, and mean, and nobody who remembers him can say just what kind of mean he was. You can match up the nature of most people with animals in the woods and either know how to get along with them or leave them alone. Nobody had ever seen a creature in the Smoky Mountains like that deputy. He ranged from simple mean to the worst kind of mean. He would dynamite fish himself, then arrest Indians just for carrying a pole out of season if they were off the reservation.

Then one night Bill shot Owl Wing Poleetika in the back. In the coroner's court, he swore it was self-defense. He said Owl Wing was hauling liquor when he stopped him and Owl Wing got out of the car and came at him with a knife, so he shot him. He said he didn't know how the bullet went in his back unless Owl Wing had swerved around as the pistol went off. In the first place, everybody knew the Poleetikas were tee-totaling, born-again Baptists, and in the second place, that they didn't own a car. One man who was in court said they didn't bring any of that up. Everybody stopped calling Bill "Spreading Adder."

Now Sam Welch never went to Bryson City and as a matter of fact didn't even come down to the village much. He kept to the mountains all the time, and sometimes some of us would go to his place and hunt with him and the others back there. Sam did not drink the strong stuff in any form nor fashion, as the man says, but when Going Home and Jonah Broken Stick and me and Big Turtle Toneed and some others used to ride horses over into Haywood County—where they had beer joints and a better class of bootlegger—then Sam would go to the boundary line of the reservation and wait for us.

The law was strict over there also and we couldn't drink in beer joints back in the 1930s. But we could always go to the bootleggers and buy white lightning. The white man named it that, and he named it right.

Some of the whites in Haywood had a harder life than the

Indians. We got to hunt and fish all year long on the reservation, but they didn't. They had to make liquor—they didn't have anything else to lean on. One other thing, talking about deputies. The ones in Haywood beat the shit out of everybody they caught drunk, white or Indian. It wasn't just Indians they picked on, like funny-eyed Bill at the bridge.

Bill just had no fit place in this world. He used to see Going Home on the bridge and yell, "Going Home, you son-of-a-bitch, you'd better go home and not come back." Or if Going Home had been drinking a little, he'd arrest him and try to bait him into resisting so he could half-kill him. Going Home always acted cowed, though, and got by. The deputy busted his head two or three times a month, but he didn't beat him up as bad as he did some of us if we bucked on him. He made some whites mad, too, and one time a white man by the name of De-Hart put a copperhead in a sack and left it in the deputy's old car. He wrecked right after he drove off, and he always blamed it on us because he said Indians knew about snakes, and white men had more sense. Another time he hit an old woman in the head with his fist because she had some snake rattles on a piece of string around her neck to keep the devil off and bring her good luck. The deputy was crazy to do that, but she was a little bit off too. It's not the rattles that keeps the dark man away, it's the snake itself.

When Bill hit the old woman, he got Sam Welch into it. Sam said that anybody who got drunk had coming whatever came, but he did not like for anything to happen to old people or children. Sam is full-blooded and he is as gentle as the wind if you know how to look at him. To this day he does not have hate or fear in his heart. I do not know why he had a white man's name. There are several families on the reservation with white-man names for reasons that go way back. Sam's wife also had what some took to be a white-man name: Moss, but in the old voice the name is Sarah-the-moss-that-grows-on-the-edge-of-the-rocks-where-the-river-throws-up-its-spray. No, Sam does not have a drop of white blood in him and he cannot speak English. He is free of fear and hate because he learned to pray in the old way—that is, with his skin and body instead of his mind and mouth. That way you can pray all the time without thinking about it and stay attached to the spirit. It is hard to tell you some of these things about Indians. First you have to know what is in the heart, then you have to translate that to the brain, then into the old tongue, and by the time you bring it into English you have lost most of it.

Sam is like a lot of Indians. When the goddamned pesky tourists come in here to gawk around and spend money at the motels that the white man owns, the old Indians stay back in the coves and ridges. Now you can talk all you want about the chiefs in the summers with their Dakota war bonnets on, and you can talk about the chiefs that the tribal council elects, but there have been precious few real chiefs around for a long time, and Sam is one of them. You can feel it. Putting titles on people don't give them authority.

He was raised up back in the big mountains. He has told me some things that all the Indians used to know. You take rattlesnakes. He has been around them all his life and he knows them. He said you can always trust a rattlesnake to do what its spirit tells it to do. He meant instinct. They got in his cabin many times and he heard them but he didn't bother them. He meant them no harm and they knew it.

After Bill hit the old woman, Sam got to where he would run down the ridges on Saturday morning and sit in the brush at the end of the bridge to study the deputy giving people a hard time. The deputy kicked one of Sam's cousins once, but Sam didn't stir. He just crouched there and watched, like he was looking at something on past the deputy, or above him, to see if the deputy's time was up yet. Sam was not going to kill him. He just wanted to see if it was the deputy's time to die—or anywhere close to it. But I can't get that across to you in English either.

Sam knew those things. One time I heard him talking to one of his boys who was getting big enough to understand. He told him the beginning of wisdom brought sorrow with it because the first wisdom is realizing that you have to die, and that even now a day is drifting toward you, like in a slow dream about yellow birch leaves falling, and that is the dying day.

The boy thought for a long time, then asked, "What are we supposed to do while we are waiting?"

Sam grinned and said, "That is the second wisdom if you can find it out. Listen to what your heart tells you and do that. Don't get drunk all the time like some of the others do. You lose track of time that way, and you need to know what has gone with all of time."

I myself am not like Going Home and some others. I like to get revenge on those who do me wrong. It is the best way because those who get to thinking about doing something to you are slow to do it if they know for a fact that you will not rest until you get even. One time Sam told me that was a bad way to think. But I cherished a desire to draw the deputy onto the reservation land on a dark night. I would have to have some help, because he was strong and mean and I was scared of him. I am not against having all the help I can get in a fight. I would like to have seven or eight holding him down good and another two or three helping me kick and beat. I used to plot up who I could get to help me if I could get "funny-eyes" onto the boundary lands. But he would not come, except with other deputies to serve state warrants. Even then, they liked to have the reservation police with them.

There are some who thought that the deputy chose an earlier day to die than the one coming for him, and that was the Saturday he fooled with Sam Welch's youngest boy. That boy had an Indian name, but he had to be a Welch on the rolls. Sam never worried one way or the other with things like that. He let them write his sons down as Joseph, Harvey, John, and Albert. But he gave them all names in the old tongue. I cannot write out the name of that youngest son but it meant the-boy-with-a-mind-like-the-air-that-goes-everywhere-and-into-the-smallest-places-as-well-as-the-big-sky. That boy did have such a mind, and when he was a small boy he reminded you of a rascal coon. He used to go across the long bridge with his grandmother about once a month, and time and again that boy saw Bill do those mean things. When he was about ten, he got a paper bag, and one night he capped it over the biggest hornets' nest he could find and tied the top closed. That Saturday he crossed the bridge with a bunch from the reservation and the bag was buzzing with angry little wings. He got to the deputy and dropped his bag. The deputy could not resist it—to stomp on some poor Indian's bag—and those hornets covered him up. He ran Sam's boy down and beat and kicked him until he broke some ribs. But Sam was out of the brush and running across the bridge like a big, mad tom turkey. He jerked the boy loose and stood and half-smiled at the deputy. Sam's eyes went into Bill's head like fangs. You could tell the deputy did not like it, but it was like a snake charming him. All the Indians gathered around close to see what would happen, and they did not care if they had to stay in jail from then on as material witnesses, because they were goddamned sure going to witness it. But all Sam did was talk softly in Cherokee.

"I know now. I do know now. I do know that there is a time coming for you and that I shall be standing there when it comes. It is going to be the worst day of all, not easy like some, and it is this that makes me not lay a hand against you at this time."

Deputy Bill did not understand a word of it. Sam lifted his boy up and carried him back across the bridge while the deputy stared like a child and rubbed his stings.

Nobody thought less of Sam for not taking revenge. He knew something about time that the rest of us had not remembered. It was ages removed from us, and from that great distance we dimly understood. Yes, even as the river runs, and the cold trees shall leaf again, even as this day comes, so also that day comes. What will we do while we wait?

This story is becoming strong in my mind now. There is a passing of years. The war came and some of us went and some did not. Sam didn't because he didn't speak English, but mainly because he didn't want to. Myself and Going Home and Big Turtle went right away to Waynesville and joined the Marines, and Jonah went to the paratroops. They say that Cherokees are not warriors by nature, but that is a goddamned lie told by fools. We all joined tough outfits—old as we were—so that in case we lived through it nobody could go around bragging that they had had it any rougher than we did.

After we got out of boot camp, they sent us to New River and put us in different companies and trained us some more. But we got to go to town some then. One day in a beer joint I ran into Going Home. They would let Indians drink beer if they were in uniform and came in with white boys. Going Home was drunk and did the happy buffalo dance when he saw me. He said it was a good thing we could get drunk now without getting our heads beat in.

"I hear funny-eyed Bill, the sonofabitch, is in the Navy," he said. "I heard they were going to draft him and he was already in trouble with a girl so he went and signed up."

We got through training at New River and they let us go home for a few days before we went overseas. Going Home, Big Turtle, and me got a train to Asheville and arrived there drunk. We got a bus out of there, and who should climb on at Waynesville but Jonah Broken Stick, who had been beat all to hell in some fight, but he was drunk and happy too. He had several pints of red-eye in his bag.

We got off at the Cherokee Bus Station, and we were high and happy and wanting to see our families. But it was far past midnight and the cafe was open, so we went in. There was just one girl at the counter and nobody else but a sailor in a white uniform, who turned out to be Bill. We sat down and looked at each other. Then we got up and circled him. I don't think anybody meant him harm—we just realized we could scare him good. He got as uneasy as we could ask, but goddamned if old good-natured Going Home didn't almost ruin it. He got tickled and was getting his bottle out to offer Bill a drink. Nobody really wanted to move on him anyway because there was a reservation policeman in a car across the road, watching us. Then the policeman got out and walked over to the cafe. Bill started to relax, but not for long. It was Sam Welch, and he walked directly in and grinned at us. Then he looked at Bill and said in Cherokee:

"I hope that you know your time is upon you and that you are comfortable in knowing it."

We sat quietly, looking at them. Then it was as if all the training in the camps had prepared us to follow Sam's orders.

"Put him in that car," Sam said in Cherokee. Going Home looked sadly at the sailor and touched his shoulder gently.

"You better go on now and get in his car," he said.

The sailor went white in the face. "No, no, no," he said. "My bus will be here in an hour. I'm not going nowhere."

Sam nodded and Big Turtle grabbed the sailor's arms and spun him out of the booth. "Don't you know by now not to give the law any trouble?" he asked. They put him in the back of the car, with Jonah on one side and Going Home on the other. The rest of us crowded into the front seat.

I have never had such a ride as in that 1936 model Ford. No one had taught Sam how to drive very good when they made him a reservation policeman. He finally made it up the highway to Wolf Creek, and by then I was sober. He kept turning around as he drove to look at Bill.

"You see that white suit he wears?" Sam said. "You could put that on over your clothes in the snow and walk up and stab a deer to death with a pocket knife."

We got to where a little trail cut off the road and Sam stopped the car. Then we all walked about a mile and a half on the trail and then went through the woods to some cliffs. It was getting daylight. There was a niche in the rocks—not a cave, but deep enough. Sam shoved the sailor in there.

"We will have to wait until the sun gets up higher," Sam said.

Jonah passed one of the pints around, but Sam shook his head. The sun was shining strong and full on the rocks now.

"They will come out now," Sam said, and climbed quickly up to a ledge about seven feet above us. When he came back down, he had a big rattlesnake in each hand. Their heads were moving all about, but they did not strike Sam. By then nobody was drunk.

"You go back to the road," Sam said, and we went. We hadn't gotten there yet when Sam put the snakes to him. We could hear all the hollering. In a little while Sam came, and he had the sailor suit rolled up.

"I will have no trouble getting many a deer wearing this," he said.

"Are you going to leave him up there?" Jonah asked in Cherokee.

"The buzzards and possums have to eat something," Sam said.

He drove us all home and told us to come and see him at the police station. He told us not to drink in the village because it was against the law and he had sworn to uphold it. He said someone would complain and he would have to lock us up.

I believe the time has come to tell the story or I would not tell it. It is funny how much you can remember when you start thinking about the old days. Now there is Going Home parading around like a chief and getting good money from the tourists, and here is me. If either one of us wants any good bear meat we have to go all the way back to Sam's place to get it. Native trout too. Once in a while we all get together and go over to the cemetery and stand around Big Turtle's grave. He won a Navy Cross and got himself killed doing it, and our village was written up in the newspapers. A lot of the older people are proud of us for being such good friends to Big Turtle before he honored himself in the war.

The
Breakaways

TIME DID NOT DRAIN HIS LIFE. IT FILLED IT
as though from a hidden reservoir with little dipping
cups. When age was upon him, virtue blossomed. Patience.
Now he let two chores consume the afternoon. In his younger
years he would have completed them in an hour, but that was
when he was in a hurry to get many things done. Patience
had gathered in him for a long time, and at last it became strong
and solid and he wondered why he had not learned it years
before. At the same time he realized that he could not have
forced the lesson in any manner.

With nothing before him for the afternoon, he sat beside his
sack of corn and with the end of a cob and his thumb he shelled
the kernels off another cob and into the bucket. The corn
spilled down effortlessly, clicking steadily as it piled on the
bottom. Age was good, now that he had reached it. Anxieties
had burned away, and now everything that he did was without
strain.

People had once bet that he would never reach twenty without someone killing him. Then, in his twenties, he got wilder
and stronger and smarter, and they began to say that someone
ought to kill him before he killed someone. But no one did,
and he killed his man and had to do a little time, but not much,
because he killed in a drunken fight with the one man in those
parts who, they said, needed killing more than he. When he
got into his thirties, the people said that he was too goddamned
mean to kill—or to die—and that he had better just be left alone.

About that time he began to think that he didn't have to

buck so hard against people or society or whatever it was that he had been fighting. He saw that his enemies would, in time, hang themselves with their own malice. He let time be the noose, but thought that he might occasionally pull at the knot. That idea grew fearsome when he began to realize that both the knot and the noose belonged to something else of a vasty nature—too much to get into his brain in one throw.

When he reached his forties, people noted that although he had taken many women, he had not taken a wife, and they said that he was going to be a mean and lonely old man when age came on. If he had ever heard them talk, he would have argued that for the most part he had been a lonely boy and a lonely young man and a lonely middle-aged man, and it then followed that he would be alone in his age. His solitude had not brought a painful loneliness, nor even emptiness. Rather it had brought freedom and privacy.

He shelled the corn, spending the afternoon with it. At dusk he walked to the pigpen and poured half of the grain into the trough. Then he walked to the little barn and poured the rest of it down the chute into the horse's trough. It was dark when he approached his house, and though he saw no men, he sensed them. Still, he was startled when a hand reached out of the blackness and grabbed him by the bib of his overalls.

"All right, now, old man. Be as quiet as you can while you tell me who else is around here," said a voice with a northern accent.

His heart pounded too fast to suit him, and fear broke in bitter buds along his tongue. But when he spoke, his voice betrayed neither excitement nor apprehension.

"There ain't nobody but me," he said. He waited, then added, "You're the three fellers who escaped the jail, ain't ye?"

"Old man, how did you know that?" The voice was less belligerent. "You got no radio or television."

The hand on his overalls loosened, and the old man stepped back.

"And how did you know that?" the man with the northern accent asked, his voice taking control.

"We already went through yore stuff, Shelton." It was the voice of a younger man that came from the darkness. Shelton knew him—the Roberts boy from Guffey Cove.

"Did you tear my place up?" the old man asked. There was push in his voice. He wanted to get the tests of will and strength underway.

"Not yet, old man," said the Roberts boy nervously. He knew Shelton's reputation. If you listened to all that had been said, half the family cemeteries in five counties held his victims.

"Well, you better not, either," Shelton said calmly.

"How come you don't have any lights here?" the northerner asked.

"The house is wired, but I like my lamps and lanterns best. I ain't generally up late."

"Well, we got that nickel-plated pistol you had in there. You got anything else in the line of guns?"

"I got a shotgun and no shells and a .22 rifle and half a box of shells," he said.

"No, you ain't. We got them now," the northerner said.

"He's got more than that, Iceman," said Roberts. "He's a mean bastard. I heard he's got 30-06s and a 30-30 up here. I've heard people say he's fired at 'em with big guns."

Shelton grinned.

"Well, if you ain't gonna kill me on the spot, let's go in."

He went inside and lit a lamp. They crowded about him and he looked at them. The oldest one was Iceman. There was wildness and danger in his eyes, but the two younger men would be the most dangerous because they didn't know what they were doing and they were scared. Shelton's legend had long ago laid hold of Roberts, and now in the presence of the old man of Big Laurel Cove, he could not keep his awe from showing. He jittered about, clawing at his face with stubby fingers. Shelton watched him.

"Yeh, ye're a Roberts, all right," Shelton said. His faint insolence was devastating.

"What do you mean by that, by God?" Roberts asked angrily.

A dim smile showed upon Iceman's swarthy features. The other escapee was as young as Roberts and looked equally unfit. He moved toward Shelton.

"Well, maybe he can just be up for murder—me and him both. If you don't watch out . . ."

His voice lacked depth, as though he feared to breathe.

Shelton stared reproachfully at him. The young one looked away, afraid of life, death, truth, time . . .

"How did you know we were the ones?" Iceman asked abruptly.

"I got a little drugstore radio. I left it at the corncrib. I was listening to the gospel music at twelve o'clock."

"What does it run on?" Iceman asked.

"One of them little batteries."

Iceman turned to the weak-voiced one.

"Parks, go get it," he said.

Parks ran out the door, came back immediately.

"What in hell is a corn crib?" he asked.

Iceman looked questioningly at Roberts.

"It's that little building down there where we saw him shelling corn," Roberts said. Roberts had taken out a big pocketknife. He scraped at his fingernails and grinned threateningly at Shelton.

The old man lowered his head. He had waited on time, and he knew that it was never enough to say you had a power or to act like you had it. You had to be the power. All Shelton had to do now was wait.

In a while Parks returned with the transistor radio, and Iceman turned it on. Country music filled the room. Shelton decided to work at small diversions.

"Don't run my battery down," he said.

Iceman stared at him. "What?" he said. "I'm ready to kill you and you're worrying about a twenty-nine-cent battery."

"Don't run the battery down," Shelton repeated mildly.

"I'll be goddamned," Iceman said, waving the pistol about threateningly. Shelton stared at him steadily, but he did not give the impression of pushing.

"For Christ's sake!" Iceman said, switching the radio off. "We'll pick up the news at ten o'clock."

Shelton built a fire in his cookstove. Then he mixed some batter, set it aside, and peeled some potatoes. He turned to Roberts and did not ask, but commanded:

"Go get me a side of meat out of the smokehouse."

Roberts obeyed without hesitation. He did not turn to Iceman for permission.

"We're going to eat, are we?" Parks asked. Iceman nodded approval. Roberts brought the meat.

"Here, let me have that knife you've got," Shelton said and reached his hand. Roberts gave him the knife. Iceman stepped forward with the pistol.

"Give it back!" he told Shelton, his eyes narrow and chill. Shelton handed it back, and Iceman turned to Roberts.

"You fool. Let me explain all of this to you. This is a jailbreak we're on. Right? Right? Now this old man here is our hostage. I don't care how old and broke-down he is, you don't just hand over the only weapon you've got to your hostage. Now, is that too heavy for you?"

Roberts struggled with the ramifications. Iceman drew back his hand, and Roberts flinched. "Jesus Christ!" Iceman said. Shelton reached above the stove, drew down a long butcher knife, and sliced the meat unnoticed.

They were eating when Iceman turned the radio on.

". . . biggest story breaking in the mountains for some time, and it's the second jailbreak at the county jail in the past two months. There had been no breaks in the jail's entire forty-year history until two months ago. It was thought to be escape-proof and many federal prisoners are kept there, awaiting trial in U.S. District Court here.

"Lawmen—including federal and state and deputies from several counties—are engaged in a massive dragnet in the area near the airport where a jailer and three other hostages have been found locked in the back of a panel truck.

"The jailer was taken hostage at gunpoint after one of the men, an accused bank robber, summoned him to his cell, then pulled out what was thought to be a small automatic pistol . . ."

The two younger escapees, absorbed in the broadcast, grinned and winked at Iceman.

". . . they stole a car and money from a man and his wife near the courthouse. Some time later the car was found abandoned near the airport. A search of the area resulted in the discovery of the jailer and the three other unidentified hostages, who appeared unharmed but refused to talk to reporters. Officers said later that the fugitives had robbed the hostages and stolen a Buick belonging to one of them. The escapees are armed and dangerous and lawmen fear that someone will be harmed unless they are found promptly. Roadblocks have been set up along highways and certain feeder roads. However, officers say it would be virtually impossible to seal up all the gravel and secondary roads which weave through the mountainous area. There is a chance that the men may yet make good their escape. Further complicating the search is the fact that at least three small planes took off from the airport at about the time the fugitives abandoned the car nearby. None of the planes filed a flight plan, and there is speculation that the escapees have either flown out or paid someone to fly them out . . ."

"He sounds like he's announcing a goddam prize fight or a touchdown or something," Iceman grunted.

". . . The escapees are identified as Shelby Parks, 20, of Greeneville, Tennessee, jailed for breaking and entering; Oscar Roberts, also 20, of Guffey Cove, North Carolina, being held for rape and violation of parole; and Richard F. 'Iceman' DeLoach of Pennsylvania, 42, who has been charged by federal authorities with bank robbery, impersonation of an FBI agent, and forging government checks and other documents. DeLoach is said to have broken out of the federal section of the jail and to have freed the others from a nearby state cell."

As soon as Iceman switched off the radio, Shelton went to bed, while the three escapees slept on the floor. When daylight came again, Shelton took a good look at them. Now he could see that Iceman's face was stony, stamped with a certain immutable malignance. There was an amoral force deep in his eyes, and if he grinned, it was with a cold, mirthless mouth. When the surface of his face moved, it seemed to move against an inner resistance, as though the face of a rutted cliff shifted from internal pressures. His two companions were callow, a mixture of fright and arrogance.

After breakfast Iceman turned on the radio. It repeated last night's news, adding a few details here and there.

". . . but the car has not yet been located, despite numerous roadblocks and checkpoints . . ."

Shelton looked up from his coffee. "Where did you put your car, by the by?" he asked.

The three were sprawled about the kitchen, and for no reason Shelton could determine, they kept watch on his lower corn field and the pasture below the barn.

"It's off that gravel road two ridges over," Iceman said. "We covered it up good so they can't see it from the air."

They stayed at Shelton's place for two more days. Then, on the third night, they went across the ridges to the car. Roberts held the big knife on Shelton while Iceman circled the car to be sure that it was not staked out.

"Now we're going to get out of here," Iceman said, "so Roberts, you better start on those road maps."

Roberts drew a line through Asheville and south through Hendersonville on the Interstate highway. In the suburbs of Asheville Iceman drove about until he spotted a newer car in a driveway. He parked the Buick in the darkness a block away.

"Come on, Parks, help me roll that one out. You keep the knife on the old man, Roberts."

Iceman and Parks stole the car quietly with no trouble—the keys were in it. They drove it back to the Buick.

"Listen," Iceman said. "I think one of us and the old man ought to ride in the trunk to keep from arousing suspicion. They're looking for three men. Besides, if the old man was up front and the cops stopped us, he might blurt out something before we could kill him. You and him get in the trunk."

"What if he tries something funny?" Roberts asked.

"Well, for Christ's sake! You've got the blade. Give 'im the blade," Iceman said.

Shelton nodded. "Yeh," he said, "you could give me the blade."

Roberts looked in the trunk. "Listen, there ain't room in here for us and the spare." He rolled the tire to the rear door and Parks put it on the back seat. Iceman was scowling.

"What in hell? If a cop stops us, what's going to look more out of place in a new car than the goddam spare on the rear seat?"

"What we gonna do?" Roberts asked.

"Throw it away."

"What if we get a flat?"

"Goddam a flat. We're running for our lives and we got five kidnap raps piled up, plus all the other charges. Don't worry about a flat. Hide that tire good. If somebody finds it, they might report it to the cops. Hurry."

"Get in," Roberts said, glowering at Shelton. He climbed into the trunk behind the old man and lay beside him. He put the knife blade flat against Shelton's chest.

"A Roberts, all right," thought Shelton. "What he don't

know about knives would fill up the sky." Iceman slammed the
trunk lid over them, and the car moved forward. Shelton
hacked Roberts on the wrist and snatched the knife from his
hand.

"Hey!" shouted Roberts.

"Son, shut up or I'll make yore mammy a pair of shoestrings
out of her darlin' boy's hide."

"Oh God! Oh God! Don't hurt me. If I ever get out of this
I'm going to get religion and change my ways," Roberts cried.

"Yeh, I guess you better. If you have to go to the walls,
somebody is gonna hurt you, son. You ain't got guts to be in
this kind of thing," Shelton said, keeping his voice easy and
soothing. He lay in the darkness and listened to the whimpers
of the young man. Sometime later the car stopped, and the
trunk was unlocked.

"Get back up here," Iceman commanded. "I can't figure out
how to drive this big airliner so well, and Parks don't even
know where second gear is. We may have to bail out in a
hurry."

Sticking to gravel roads, they dodged two roadblocks, then
got into the clear on the Interstate. At dawn they left the
big highway and drove on secondary roads until they
found an old church. Parking behind it, they napped, roused
to listen to the radio, napped again. Late in the afternoon
they moved on, stopping once at a small restaurant for food.
Dark was falling when they crossed the state line into South
Carolina.

"Oh boy!" Roberts said, "we're outta the state now. They
ain't looking for us here. We're outta bad trouble."

Iceman stared at him, a grim smile on his face.

"Listen, sonny boy. They're looking for us everywhere,
and we're into bigger trouble than ever, if you want to measure
it that way."

Roberts stared at him in disbelief.

"We've got a kidnapped man with us, right?" Iceman asked.

"Yeh? So what? We had him all the time."

"We just crossed a state line with him."

"What?" he asked. "So what?"

"Federal. It's federal now. Death penalty. They don't let up until they get you."

Roberts began to whimper, and Parks clutched his stomach.

"Oh God! Oh good God," Parks said.

Iceman met Shelton's eye in the dying daylight.

"Consequently, old man, we won't have to pay any more if we do have to kill you. You just think about that from now on."

"Yeh. That shore is something to think about," Shelton said. "Ye're snakebit and gonna die anyhow. You wouldn't have nothing to lose, would you?"

Iceman laughed bitterly, and the two younger men shrank in terror.

"I've got plenty of federal raps anyway," Iceman said.

"Well, I ain't," Roberts said. "You turn this car around and let's take him back home."

"Too late now," Iceman said. "We've already brought him across. It don't matter how many times we take him back, we've busted the cherry now."

The two younger men began to gabble between themselves. Iceman watched them in the rear-view mirror. "Jesus!" he snorted, "We're three rough and desperate criminals, all right. Yessir, I threw in with the toughest and meanest of the lot when I left."

He drove wearily.

Rain began to fall; heavy blobs caught and spattered on the windshield, were slung away by the wipers. In the night the radio suddenly glowed at Iceman's touch, and an announcer said that the stolen Buick had been found near Asheville. There was no information on the newer stolen car. Once the car skidded a bit on a slick spot, then steadied. A police car came in sight in front of them, its blue blinker whirling madly. They all leaned forward, but the car shot past them, heading northward.

"On their way to set up a roadblock at the state line," Iceman said tersely.

"I can't stand much more of this," Roberts said. Parks sobbed.

"You're going to have to stand it the rest of your life," Iceman snorted. "Do you know how long the rest of your life is? Well, you'll have to keep on running."

Shelton nodded his head. Iceman too, he saw, knew about time.

"I didn't mean to get in this far," Roberts said.

"Well, here you are. One of the most wanted men in eight states. A helluva promotion for you boys. A petty thief and an ordinary rapist have now been elevated to the ranks of kidnappers, robbers, and maybe murderers. Think of it. If they get us alive we'll all be on Death Row together and get to know some really interesting people."

Roberts suddenly sat up. The worst of his panic was gone. "Eight states, eh? How do you know?"

"They always used to say 'eight-state alarm.' It's probably more than that now," Iceman said. Parks was crying, but Roberts sat back and lit a cigarette. His voice was suddenly strong and assured.

"Why, they don't know what three bad-asses they've let loose," he said.

The car seemed a vast, silent compartment hurtling through rain and darkness. By midnight they had cut back into North Carolina and were two hundred miles east of Asheville. They stopped once at an all-night service station. Iceman had settled down some. When his two younger comrades went to the rest room, he turned to Shelton.

"Don't act funny or I'll have to hurt you. But I want you to know there's nothing personal in this. I decided you're a good old cooter."

"Ah, you don't have to worry about me," Shelton said. "I'd worry about them, if it was me in your place. They're scared to death. Either of 'em or both of 'em might decide they could get a deal if they gave you and them up and told . . ."

"What?" Iceman said. "Shut up, now. They better not . . ."

But the wedges were in the crack. Shelton sat back.

Later in the night they stopped at another restaurant and ate. At dawn they checked into a motel in Newport News, Virginia. Inside, Iceman flopped onto a bed and untied his shoes. Then he slipped off his shirt and pants and threw them to Roberts.

"Hang these up. We got to get some new clothes."

"I'm hungry," Roberts said. He turned to Shelton. "What do you say, old man?" His tone was friendly, ingratiating. The other youth had also shown a change of attitude toward Shelton. His unassertive influence with these two was spreading, and authority was tilting his way. But he was wise with it. Authority had its own life and presence. He merely let it roost on him, as a bird roosts in a tree.

Shelton shrugged.

"Well, do you think we ought to get some more food or not?" Roberts asked.

Iceman jerked up from the bed, his eyes flashing.

"I'd like to know just who is running this jailbreak?" he said. "Yes, go get some food. Hell, go out and get caught. But when you do, let me tell you, you better hope they kill you before you tell them where I am. Good Christ! All right. Go get some sandwiches. Parks can stay here and keep an eye on the old man while I sleep."

He handed the pistol to Parks, rolled over, and hid his head under the pillow. Parks took the gun, grinned wickedly, waved it around, and pointed it for a moment at Shelton. The old man stared it down. Iceman was snoring.

Parks put the pistol down on the dresser, went into the bathroom, and sat on the commode. Shelton moved so he could look through the half-opened door. He did not believe what he saw. Parks's face reflected a holy air of prayer and suffering. Shelton picked up the pistol and waved it. Parks did not notice.

Shelton thought over the pattern of his life. He had killed over a trifle and in a temper. As time passed, he had known regret and had come to see how worthless it was to kill. Wisdom accumulated slowly. If it took the regret of killing one man to keep from killing again, then perhaps it was well. He thought upon the sleeping Iceman, who did not seem to be a killer despite all. Then he slipped the old lead cartridges out of the pistol. It did not take him long to poke them into the crack below the hinge on the bathroom door and bend the leads out of the casings. He poured the powder from each casing into his pocket and stuck the lead firmly back into the casing. Now, even if Iceman were tempted to kill, he would fail. He put the pistol back where Parks had left it. When the young man came out of the bathroom, he stared at the pistol, then at Shelton. The old man returned the stare and lay down across the other bed and slept.

Iceman's insane screaming soon awakened him.

"You what? You what?"

"Well, I didn't see no harm in it," Roberts said.

"You didn't see no harm in it? I guess you don't see no harm in us all getting the gas chamber four times apiece," Iceman shrieked. He had the pistol pointed at Roberts' stomach. Roberts' fearful eyes turned to Shelton, who stared back impassively.

"What's he done?" Shelton asked.

"I ought to blow his goddamned heart out. He called his whore of a wife on the long distance telephone."

"Now wait a minute, by God," Roberts protested. Parks backed off in a corner, his face white.

"Wait a minute? You idiot. You son-of-a-bitch, you whore-mongering rapist son-of-a-bitch . . ."

"What's the harm in it?" Shelton asked.

"Nothing, except that by now the cops and the feds are on their way here to get us. You know they're bound to have your ol' lady's house staked out and taps on the phone. Come on, let's go. Let's get out."

By noon they were approaching Arlington, tired, bickering.

Passing into the city's outer ring of motels, they could not decide...

Shelton decided for them. "This'n looks good," he said. "Jist pull in here."

Iceman pulled in and stopped. Then he looked around darkly at Shelton. "I'll be damned," he said. "Are you sure this one will suit you, your honor?"

Having obeyed, he could not now refuse. Besides, the two youths were out of the car stretching. Iceman, humiliated in some subtle fashion, walked to the office and checked in. They all slept immediately. Much later Shelton raised his head, watched them for a while, then fell back into slumber. When they awakened at last, it was after dark and the two young men were wanting liquor.

"Booze? Stupids. It's hard enough with you two sober. Christ A'mighty, I catch you with booze and I'll shoot both of you," Iceman said.

Parks went for food. They ate, then ran again. This time they drove west, leaving a twisty track for anyone who might try to predict their movements. Shelton commented on the route, and their response was one of pleasure at his approval. Shelton was sitting in the front seat with Iceman, staring straight ahead. Once they stopped for gasoline shortly before dawn. Iceman and Parks went to the rest room.

"Let 'im have it with that blade if he tries anything," Iceman told Roberts. But as soon as they were out of sight, Roberts turned to Shelton.

"Listen, Mr. Shelton. Let's you and me get outta here. You can tell the law that I didn't want to come but Iceman and Parks made me break out with them. You can turn me in. I don't want you to cut me with that knife. You don't have to do that. If you stay on with 'im, Iceman might kill you."

"I don't believe he wants to hurt me," Shelton said.

By dawn they were in a motel in Maryland. They slept, awakened to bicker, fled again into the highways. Then another town, another dawn. The sameness was wearing upon everyone except Shelton. Under his slouched hat he watched, waited, now and then taking silent command, then fading again. They awakened from a sleep at midday, and Iceman sent the younger ones out for food. Darkness came and they had not returned. Iceman howled about the rooms.

"They've deserted. The punks. The goddam punks. If I could get my hands on them . . ." he said bitterly.

He paced the floor, scowling, studying the walls, sat down, leaped up to pace again, muttering, oblivious of the old man. Shelton sat unmoving in a chair. He felt the stirring of something dark and inevitable, as if he had waited and studied all his life and the final answer was going to come to him in small pieces.

It was late when Parks shouted at the door.

Iceman threw open the door and jerked him inside. He stuck the pistol in his stomach.

"Where you been? Goddam you, where you been? Where you been? I'm going to kill you. Where's that other punk? Where? I said where?"

He struck Parks in the face with the pistol, raking his cheek with the sight at the end of the barrel. Blood welled and gushed down the frightened face.

"That's what I came to tell you. We went and got some sandwiches. On the way back we saw this woman walking along. He pulled over and made her get in. I told him you'd be mad, but he said he had to have it. He liked the way she was walking. It got him going. He drove out to an old schoolhouse. That's when I got out and run. I like to never have found this place."

Iceman slumped back. He pounded his forehead with the heel of his hand. "A rapo. You can't break 'em. They'll do it every time. Goddam it, I knew that. I knew it."

He sat hunched for a time, then straightened.

"Well, we've got to steal another car. I counted up my

money, and there's only about a hundred left. We're going to have to stick up a bank."

Parks's face turned paler, the bloody streak showing vivid, unreal.

"Listen, let's split up that money, Iceman," he whined.

"What? You're outta your bean. This is my money. I just invited you guys along."

"Yeh, but I thought . . ."

"Thought?" Iceman's face was a tight mask. "Listen, man. I don't want you to start trying to think now. You are a punk who could endanger the world if you started trying to think. Thinking takes a lot of time and practice, and you just ain't conditioned to it or equipped for it. Why don't you start off easy until your mind gets used to it? You might screw yourself up if you got a real thought going."

Parks sat back in misery. It was a short time later when they heard a car pull up in the parking place outside. Iceman jerked the pistol out and stood beside the door. It was Roberts.

"Iceman. Let me in. I got the chow."

Iceman cracked the door, reached out, and jerked Roberts in. Sandwiches and cartons of milk fell to the floor when Iceman hit him.

"What happened to that woman?"

Roberts grinned. "She liked it."

"Where is she?"

"Ah hell, Iceman. She's a nothin' . . ."

Iceman slapped him again.

"All right. All right," Roberts said. "I beat her up and left her there."

He started to cry.

"Did you kill her? Did you hurt her bad?"

"No! God no, Iceman."

Iceman became as calm as a pond. Shelton leaned forward a bit.

"Give me that goddamned knife," Iceman said to Roberts.

"I can't. I lost it," Roberts sniffled.

"You left it in that woman . . ."

Roberts looked at Shelton. The old hat had been shoved back and Shelton's face was clear, young-old, his eyes alive with power.

"He's got it," Roberts sobbed. Iceman turned and looked at Shelton.

"How long has he had it?"

"Since that night you made us get in the car trunk in Asheville."

Iceman held out his hand. Shelton smiled with regret. He handed over the knife, even as he realized what Iceman was going to do. A force was in the room, a terrible dark force, brimming over. Iceman opened the knife, took a quick step, and stabbed Roberts in the stomach, angling the knife up at the end of his thrust until he pierced the heart. His hand turned red in the flood, and Roberts fell dead. Parks watched with a child's puzzlement.

"I knowed you was going to do that, but I still wasn't ready for it," Shelton said.

Iceman looked sadly at him. "I felt his heart give its last beat out there at the end of the knife."

Parks arose, troubled of face. He tottered to the door, opened it, and ran away. Iceman did not move. Shelton arose and shut the door. Then he sat again, and all night he looked from the corpse to Iceman and studied his own mind. Before daylight came Iceman got up.

"Come on. We've got to put some distance between us and this place. Jesus Christ! Rape and murder and what all else . . ."

Shelton followed him to the car. False dawn was upon the city. Shelton marveled at the quality of the light from a remote and sleepy place in his mind. They drove to a restaurant and stopped. Before they went in, Iceman leaned to Shelton.

"Old man, if you do the wrong thing, I'll kill you."

The old man nodded. Suddenly he leaned forward to stare at an early newspaper in a rack a few feet away. The picture showed Parks, dead in a pool of blood, a few feet from the broken glass door of a store. A loaf of bread and some cans were strewn around him.

"Get us that paper, Iceman. Parks has been killed."

"What?" Iceman shouted in disbelief. He went to the rack and took out the paper. The headline read, "Burglar Killed in Midnight Gunfight with Cops."

Iceman read aloud angrily:

"A young man, unidentified at deadline, was shot and killed by police about midnight when he tried to shoot his way out of a food store he had broken into, according to a police desk sergeant.

"Police said he carried no identification. However, they said they feel his death solves several burglaries and armed robberies here, dating back several months.

"Officers said the young man, surprised inside the store, reached for his gun and ran out the door at the same time. He was hit by several police bullets. Spokesman said that impressions of the slain man's fingerprints would be forwarded to FBI headquarters in Washington to see if they are on file there."

"Man, he didn't have a gun. I don't think he even knew how to use one," Iceman said.

"I know," Shelton said.

"Goddam, I'm blowing this town. This is a den of murderers in uniform," Iceman said. Slowly they went inside and sat at a table. The waitress came, standing tiredly.

"Bring us eggs and sausage and coffee," Iceman said.

Exhaustion opened a deeper mind in Shelton. He stared out the window at the empty street, the scene at once vivid and strong, dim and vague—frozen in his mind and yet moving like the slow run of a brook near his house as it flowed from under the bridge. He envisioned Iceman dead. They ate quickly and quietly. Then Shelton said apologetically:

"I have to go home now, Iceman."

"What?" Iceman demanded, shaking his head, not comprehending. "How would you like also to get your ass killed?"

Shelton's mind shifted. Something had a hold on him and was gently pulling, pulling, pulling. He thought . . . death is coming on a day and in a manner not yet known, coming at its own speed.

"I said take me home, Iceman. I have to go and you have to take me."

Iceman stared a moment, then nodded. Shelton arose and walked to the car.

The journey was mostly silent but tense. After five hours Iceman began crying softly. Shelton turned and looked at him in a gentle way.

"I don't know what's happened," Iceman said. "I knew all along it was a mistake to take you. When I first went with that Roberts on your land, I felt everything was wrong. Now they're dead. I felt something scary all along, and it gets worse. I don't want to hurt you, old man. I feel toward you like I did about an uncle I once had. He was the only one in my life who didn't come at me sideways or raising hell or wanting something. When I went to his funeral, I felt things I never could talk about, and I feel 'em about you."

Shelton nodded gently. The car sped south along the highway. Again the silence. They ate and gassed up and traveled on, and as they did, a sense of relief seemed to come over Iceman.

"Listen, old man Shelton," he said, "everything ain't gonna be all right. Nothing has ever been all right. Somebody'll kill my ass, or they'll lock me up for a long time. Neither one of them things is all right. I ain't got nowhere to go. Not even a grave to get buried in, you know. That's a sad state of affairs, but it dawned on me that's the way it is. But if I ever get clear, I'd like to come back and visit you, if you don't mind."

Shelton smiled gratefully.

"Feel at home. Come anytime," he said.

It was past daylight when Iceman pulled the car up the old road to Shelton's place and stopped. They stared at each other tiredly.

"Well, adios, old man Shelton."

"Come in and rest."

"No. Someday. Right now I want to be as far from you as I can get, and I don't know why."

He gunned the motor, pulled off. Shelton had his shoes off and was sitting on the edge of his bed when he heard the shotgun blasts down by the bridge. He sighed deeply, plucked at a sharp toenail, then walked through the pasture and beside the brook down to the bridge. A frightened young deputy stood back from where Iceman's body had fallen into the little run as it rilled out from under the bridge.

"Who in the hell is this crazy bastard, Mr. Shelton?" the young man asked.

"I believe him to be one of the ones who broke out of the jail a few days ago."

The deputy stood back, his riot gun still pointed toward the body.

"The hell he is? Them other two been killed up north. That was just on the sheriff's radio and all. How come he was here?"

"They carried me off and then this one brought me back just a while ago. He weren't a bad man."

"The hell he weren't. You see that pistol?" the deputy's toe pointed to Shelton's nickel-plated pistol lying just under the stolen car.

"I stopped to let him by. I had no idea who he was. I was coming to see if you'd let me keep some game roosters up here. He pulled up even with me and leaned out of that car and snapped that iron at me. I nearly shit. I never seen anybody look that mean in my life, snapping that little gun in my face. I dropped my own pistol and kicked it under the seat trying to pick it up. I thought I never would get my shotgun stuck out my window. He was out of his car coming at me and I blowed him down into the creek."

Shelton sat in the grass and looked at the blasted flesh and bone of Iceman's chin and neck, and watched the little worms of blood curl and crawl in the cold water.

"You got to get him to the undertaker, I guess," Shelton said. "You tell 'em I said he can have a grave up here on my place. You bring them roosters on anytime you want to."

The deputy spoke into his radio, explaining to his office.

Something filled and emptied, drained away, began another slow accumulation. Shelton pulled Iceman's head and shoulders onto the bank of the little creek, then walked slowly to his place and fed his chickens before he went to sleep.

Larse's
Place

THE CHAMBER OF COMMERCE, NEEDING AN
impressive name, began to call the highway across the
mountains the Eastern Gateway. Along the route the ramparts
of the Great Smoky Mountains can be seen rising, sometimes
above the clouds. Mountains that once deterred early settlers
and travelers do so no longer. They are speedily traversed by
tourists, who swarm into the area beginning in the spring of
the year. All summer and into the autumn they come to see
the far-thrown mountain ranges, and they see little else.

Larse Weems ran the little clapboard shack on the eastern
side of the mountain that served as the "last chance" to buy
candy bars and drinks before the road crossed the gap and ran
into the reservation. The store had once had a name, but the
sign bearing it had been shot away. A few hundred feet below
Larse's place was a sign marking "The Most Photographed
View in the Smokies," but the mountain hoojers and the
Indians had shot so many holes in it that no one could even tell
if the spelling was right. Not only was that sign shot up, but
every highway department sign within fifteen miles had been
well sprinkled, usually during the bursts of high spirits that
came from drinking the moonshine that Larse sold. Some signs
had caught loads of birdshot that only made dents, some had
bigger dents and holes from buckshot, and from there you
could go right on up the range of calibers—.22, .25, .32, 30-30,
.38, .38 Special, 30-06, and .44. Almost everyone from the
east side of the mountain—the white hoojers and the breeds
from Haywood—could tell who had done the shooting by the

size of the hole. They made it their business to know exactly what kind of gun a person might have in the bib of his overalls or in his truck. Such knowledge could come in handy when "discussions" heated up.

As the highway looped and twisted up the east side of the mountain, on one side the mountain itself sloped down almost to the edge of the pavement, but on the other side there was a void—a long drop to the valley below. At one stretch, from high up, the silvery ribbon of Roaring Creek could be seen. And way back at its headwaters was located the still of an independent mountain supplier, a man known to only a few. Larse was one of the few. He got his moonshine there, and selling the illegal liquor was how he made his money. Once a week a delivery was made to Larse—always in the darkest hour before dawn. Larse knew perfectly well that the law wouldn't waste the best hour for a stakeout on a small operator like himself. Early morning raids were reserved for the big dealers.

Even though Larse had no sign on his place, his customers generally referred to it—with a certain wry wit—as the "Overhang," since the rear section was built on tall poles and the drop-off in the back was deep. In front a planked porch, which faced a small graveled area off the highway, was scuffed and splintered from the tread of hobnailed boots. The flooring inside bore the same marks.

Larse lived alone in two small rooms under the main floor, and that was where he slept when he closed up shop. If the store was closed more than two days running, Larse's customers sought other watering holes because they knew that he had found one of the consignments to his liking and had elected to drink it rather than sell it.

This one was a four-day stupor. When Larse finally roused himself, he drank a pint for the snakes and shakes, then reopened his store. The word went out slowly that Larse was back to himself. His customers were faithful, trusting in the quality of his "herbs." Larse sat on the rickety porch, looking like hell-before-breakfast, but it was not unnoticed that he was open for business.

He blinked his watery eyes in the strong light after days underground. He was wiry, his shoulders hunched from the load of his years. He had lost his plates, and his mouth was sunken. In some past year, remote in his memory, he had succumbed to thick spectacles, which magnified the pale weakness of his distrustful eyes. Unshorn gray hair, as thick and tough as a wild boar's pelt, stuck from under his cap.

He sunned until the early afternoon, pondering the folly of drinking liquor and watching with disinterest as tourist cars screamed around the curve above his place, straightened, and roared on down the mountain. They almost never stopped here, and he was not interested in attracting them. Once he had tried a tourist line, some plaster Indian heads and Jesuses, but his regular customers had shot them to pieces. Now he did not deal with tourists.

"Flatland sons-of-bitches," he said.

Suddenly Larse left his chair, eased apprehensively to the edge of the porch, and stared up the road. Then he went inside. Three breeds from the reservation were filing along the side of the highway. Larse didn't like to see them coming. They acted worse than the hoojers when they got to drinking.

They came straight across his porch, looking slyly at Larse from liquid eyes. Two were tall and angular, one with a deeply pocked face—evenly spaced craters like aboriginal tattoos—and the other with a long, sharp nose like an eagle's beak. The third Indian was younger—squat, with a mass of mahogany flesh for a face, and narrow, suspicious eyes.

"Well, what do you boys want?" Larse asked, hating it that his voice cracked under the strain of his hangover. They leaned forward against the makeshift counter of raw pine boards covered with splintered plywood.

"You got any likker, Larse?" the big-nosed one asked respectfully.

"You got any money?" countered Larse, his eyes narrow.
"Yes."

"Lemme see it."

The man glanced at the short one and nodded. Sullenly the
shorter one pulled out a worn chaingang wallet and opened it
almost defiantly, revealing four one-dollar bills.

"How much likker you boys want?" Larse asked.

They looked at one another, talking with their eyes and a
few twist-tongue words.

"Give us three seventy-five-cent drinks," said the one with
the eagle's beak.

Larse set up three large, clean snuff glasses on the counter
and poured them full from a half-gallon jar. The Indians
watched, fascinated by the sparkling moonshine. For their
benefit, Larse held up the jar and shook it. They watched
carefully, judging the quality of the liquor by the foam on
top.

"Well, so this good likker, then Larse?" asked the talking
one in the half-interested way of a pre-drinking conversation,
a thirsty eye on his glass.

"Yessir! Yer damn right it is. You seen that bead yeself. I
don't sell nothing but the best I can get," Larse said proudly.

"Give us a grape dope to chase it with," the Indian said,
placing three one-dollar bills on the counter. Larse gave him
the *Grapette* and the change, and the short one scooped the
coins into his wallet.

Eagle-nose got half his drink down, slugged the chaser,
gagged, and handed the chaser on, his eyes filled to overflow-
ing. Then they all drank in turn, nodding and praising the quality of the liquor. Larse shifted his eyes to the passing tourist cars,
uncomfortable with his hangover and the presence of the un-
predictable breeds. As the lull lengthened, Larse felt in them a
subtle, silent shifting of mood.

"You boys didn't walk all the way up here from the village,
did you?" he asked.

The talkative eagle-nose shook his head, relaxing a bit. "Naw," he said, his voice tinged with the accent of the Appalachian whites, "I like likker all right, but I wouldn't walk fifteen miles up that mountain for two barrels of it and a mule and a wagon to haul it in."

The tedium of the summer afternoon wore on, and the silence held a spirit that Larse could detect but could not identify. Whether the mood was friendly or threatening, whether it would break out in song and dance or in murder or robbery, he couldn't tell. The Indians rolled cigarettes and leaned against the counter to smoke and sip on the moonshine. If a car slowed on the road outside, they obligingly slid their glasses toward Larse so he could hide them under the counter. As their tongues loosened, the two tall ones began to murmur together in low conversation.

"You been layin' up with Nellie?" asked the one with the pockmarks, a polite interest in his voice.

"Well, yeh. I go see her some," snickered the eagle-nosed one.

"How is that stuff?" asked the other.

"What you mean? What stuff?" eagle-nose asked evasively, then snickered and finally laughed loudly, swinging away from the bar in an impromptu little dance.

"I mean how is that stuff? Man, I ain' had any in so long I forgot what it's like."

"You ought to go get some, then."

"Huh! The only ones I know want to be kept up or get married. You tell me what it's like."

"It's good and warm," eagle-nose said, draining his glass and grimacing. "Whew! Whew!" he snorted.

"Is it comfortable in there?" asked the pock-marked man, who suddenly began to giggle idiotically.

"Well, get yourself a girl and find out," eagle-nose said.

The squat Indian suddenly grunted in exasperation. He had held his silence in great, absorbing introspection, contemplating the madness of the liquor in his brain. A wild light flashed through his slitted eyes. He pounded his pudgy fist on the bar in an insistent drumbeat. Larse looked momentarily at a pistol lying on a shelf under the bar, then looked away.

"When you seen Alex Bradley?" the short one demanded. "He's supposed to be the baddest ass in the valley."

Larse shook his head, pressing his lips together. His hand began to tremble. He had sworn several times that he would never again sell liquor to an Indian.

"Lissen. Alex Bradley ain' bad. Somebody just tol' him that and he started believing it," the short man said. "He's been comin' over on the boundary tryin' to get our women, and I'm gonna break him of that habit."

"Alex Bradley is hard to handle," Larse croaked weakly, glowering and uneasy. "I've seen him do his stuff."

"I've beat him. I've whupped him all over hell, ain' I?" the short Indian asked the tall ones, who were swaying about in a half-trance. They looked stupidly at him.

"Well, ain' I?"

Finally the liquid pools of their eyes focused. Both shrugged slightly—with him, but not quite all the way.

"You know damn well I did—you know I did, don't you?" the short one insisted, furious that his companions would not throw their entire and enthusiastic support behind his claim. He pounded on the bar again. The tall ones were amused.

"Yeh, yeh," they said together.

"I ain' ever seen the man from Maggie Valley I couldn't whup," the short, paunchy Indian declared, thumping himself on the chest with his fist. Larse kept a wary, speculative eye on him. His thin old shoulders twitched. His sunken mouth pressed together in a grim, knotty line, bringing his chin almost to his nose.

"You got high pretty damn quick, didn't you?" Larse asked him.

"To hell with you, old man. You give us a drink, huh?"

Larse picked up the jar, more for want of something to do with his hands than anything else.

"I'll sell you a drink," he said.

"Whatju say? What was it you said?" The pig eyes narrowed more and the fat fist began to flex.

"You got money. I'll sell you a drink," Larse whispered, his mouth dry.

"Why don't you just up and give us a drink out of the goodness in your heart, you goddam white son-of-a-bitch?"

Larse began to tremble, mad and frightened. He looked again at the pistol. The belligerent man was pounding on the counter again. Larse shook his head sadly and sighed: "Listen, the government would lock me up if they knew I sold likker to you boys."

"What ju think they might do if they found out you helped pay for and operate that still up on Roaring Creek, Larse?" The short man guffawed.

Larse winced. "How did ye know about that?" he asked.

The two tall Indians stood watching impassively, bending neither to this wind nor to that, but keeping a track on the proceedings.

"If the government don't know you sell us likker, Larse, they're the only ones. Besides, that law ain' no good no more. We can drink anytime we want to. So you just hand over a free drink to your good ol' friends, huh?" he asked craftily. A panther toying with a staked goat.

Larse studied his adversary a second, then looked at the other two, who now hovered in a dark, inscrutable threat.

"All right! All right, sir! All right, by God!" Larse said in grandiose and bitter concession. "I'm a-goin' to give you one." And he hated himself for it.

The three of them crowded up to the counter, their dark eyes glittering with amusement and high triumph.

"You pour it the same size as the ones we pay you money for, Larse," the victor demanded loudly, grinned, and stared all about in feigned idiocy.

Larse poured the liquor, brimful, into the glasses.

"That's the way to act, old man. You do like we say. We're three of the meanest goddam people you'll ever see," crowed the short one.

"You get drunk and out-of-the-ordinary awful fast," Larse sniffed in defeat.

The other laughed uproariously. "You ain' supposed to give us the likker to get so drunk on. Why, we're dangerous as hell and we don't give a shit for nothing."

His comrades snickered at the sport.

Eagle-nose gave way to exhilaration. He laughed insanely and leaped to the middle of the rough floor. His long legs bent to a slight crouch. He held his arms stiffly, one forward and one back, at a ninety-degree angle. The pock-marked one, holding unsteadily to the plywood top of the counter, expelled his breath in a long, tired whoosh. The tall man in the middle of the room was weaving sinuously and pumping his arms like pistons.

"You see that, Larse?" asked the short one. "He's gettin' ready to do the friendship dance, and when he starts that, it means the friendship is over. He might take your scalp. That's what all you whites think. That's what happens when you sell firewater to the redman. We might just decide to tear down your place and go on the warpath down through Maggie Valley."

Larse glowered, helpless, as the man unbuttoned his shirt and stuck out his paunchy stomach. "You see that chest, Larse. Like a bull's. I'm as hard as a rock. I'm so goddam hard and mean I might decide to kill you."

Larse looked at the fat rolling over the other's belt.

"Oh hell fire," he said in disgust, looking beyond the Indian to the outside, where an out-of-state car was pulling into the parking area. Without looking around, the Indian muttered "State Patrol," and the three of them froze in place for a moment, then clustered at the bar, staring in stupefaction at the blank boards of the wall behind it. The short one wrapped his hand around the grape bottle as if he had been nursing a soft drink.

The tourist honked his horn. Larse ignored him, watching instead the three Indians. Finally he looked through the window at the car, which held a man, a woman, and two children. The horn stopped blowing and a small man with bulging, impatient eyes walked inside.

"Do you sell gasoline here?" he barked, curling his lips in disgust at the rude interior and the odors of shellac, resin, tar, and liquor. He ignored the Indians, who still stared blankly at the wall.

"D'ye see any goddam gas pumps out there?" snapped Larse.

The tourist was startled, immediately intimidated.

"No, sir," he answered meekly.

"Well, that's because I don't sell gas," Larse said.

The flatlander stood, embarrassed, unable to do the next thing, whatever it might be. Finally he cleared his throat and croaked, 'Well, sir, do you sell Cokes here?"

"Yep," Larse said. The three Indians had turned to stare fiercely at the tourist, their heads bowed forward from their shoulders like three attentive, hungry vultures.

"Please, give me four, please. How much are four Cokes?" the wayfarer whimpered.

All right, now, Larse thought, what is going out of one pocket ought to be coming back to the other pocket. He had been bullied out of three good-sized horns of liquor. Taking four Cokes from the cooler, he set them on the counter and said, "Four Cokes will be two dollars."

"What? Two dollars for four Cokes? My God . . ."

The Indians had straightened and were examining the tourist as though he might have been a rare and interesting species of bird lately flown into their trees. For the time being, their allegiance had shifted to Larse.

"All right. All right. Give me the four, please," the little man said, and in his voice was the resignation of a long-suffering traveler in strange lands.

Before uncapping the Cokes, Larse opened the drink box again and got one for himself, setting it under the counter next to the pistol. Then he turned to the tourist and said, "If ye keep the bottles that'll be twenty cents extra."

"We'll leave the bottles outside," said the tourist grimly. "How much will it cost me to find out how far it is to the next service station?"

"Two more dollars and we'll guide you there," said the squat Indian brightly.

"It's a half a mile down the mountain and it don't cost you nothing to learn that," Larse said. The tourist got to the door, turned, and asked angrily, "How much do they charge for Cokes down there?" Then he scurried out to his car. Larse and his customers watched through the dirty window as the family drank down the Cokes quickly. They dropped the bottles on the ground and spun gravel as they left. The three Indians converged on Larse.

"Listen Larse, while you was getting him, why in hell didn't you tell him he could get three real Indian chiefs to pose for pictures for a quarter apiece?"

Larse grinned weakly, reached for his Coke, and took a sip. The squat Indian hummed a few bars of a Hank Williams tune, and the tall ones went back to the center of the floor, striking their war dance pose. Then the squat one thrust his stomach through his shirt again.

"You see that build, Larse? And I'm as mean as a big old rattlesnake, on top of being built so good. I might just tear your face up and then go down into the valley and whup Alex Bradley right good, and show his old lady what a good time is. You believe me, Larse? Don't you believe I'll beat hell out of you?"

He reached across the counter and grabbed the front of Larse's shirt. Larse's hand dropped and closed on the pistol.

"Well, I wouldn't even think about sich shit as that if I was you, big chief," Larse said coldly.

The other was baffled and shook his brutish head, but the arrogance remained in his eyes. The dancers had stopped weaving and watched with interest. The squat one released his hold and reeled back from the counter. He closed his fists and set his feet in the stance of a bad boxer. He was amazed at the impudence of the old man.

"Why not? Why wouldn't I think about it?" he asked.

"I'm now good and tired of being bullied in my own place. You open your mouth one more time, fat ass, and I'm going to blow a hole in you that I can bury your two friends in," Larse croaked, his weak eyes ashine and his knotty lips grinning wickedly.

"Yeh, what with?" the Indian asked cautiously.

Larse brought the pistol up and into view. He pulled back the hammer and whirled the cylinder. The wild light disappeared from the Indians' eyes and was replaced by expressions of respect and perplexity. They stood in shocked and embarrassed silence. There was nowhere for this conversation to go next. For a long time, they all stood as they were. Suddenly, eagle-nose brightened and turned the personality on.

"How about selling us another drink, Larse old boy? Three twenty-five-cent shots will be all right."

The squat one was absorbed in buttoning his shirt, rolling his thick tongue around his lips like a child just reprimanded. Larse stuck the pistol under his belt, picked up the fruit jar, and poured a small amount—a few drops—in each glass and took the money.

The pock-marked one stared at the diminished drinks. "That's a quarter drink?" he inquired cautiously. Larse had the pistol back out, spinning the cylinder. They reached for the drinks without gesture or word and quickly drained them.

Larse had turned away from them and looked at a distant curve down the highway. He could see a man on the shoulder of the road, walking up the mountain toward them.

"Well, big chief," Larse said, his pale eyes triumphant and his chin almost joining his nose, "here comes Alex Bradley himself. You'll never get a better chance at him."

Then he grinned hugely and cackled loudly. "He carries a Case Double X with a five-inch blade, and its like a razor. He's cut several in here. They tell me he'll cut you to ribbons over nothing. Ain't no telling what he'll do if you make him mad."

The Indians stared at the man coming up the road. The eagle-nosed one straightened and looked toward Soco Gap. "My friends," he said formally, "the shadows grow long. We had better go up the mountain before dark."

Together they raised their empty glasses to see if another drop might be drained.

"That's real good likker, Larse," eagle nose said respectfully, belched courteously, and headed for the door.

"Yeh it is, Larse," said the pocked one, following.

"Take care of yourself, Larse old boy," the squat one said from the door. Larse watched them go single file up the shadowed road—the eagle-nosed one walking in front with dignity, the pock-marked one lurching along, and the one with the pig eyes running on short, unsteady legs to keep up.

The Blue Glint of a Queen's Last Jewel

TODAY THE RHYTHMS OF LEXINGTON Street were soft and restrained because the weather was building. Sky and wind blended clouds and mixed them in thin layers, and the drunks, derelicts, cheap merchants, and rummage shop operators went about like the fowl of the land making ready for the storm to blast down upon them. Their energies were banked like fires. Their eyelids drooped low and they did not smile. The air pressure was strange and the derelicts responded to it with sensitive, inner barometers. Professor Parker wondered whether such reactions might have something to do with the way their lives had splintered. As a sociologist, he rejected no possibility, no matter how implausible.

He was half a block down Lexington when they spotted him and waved tentatively from various doorways and overhangs. Big Nell sat hunched on an old crate at the end of the passageway to an old, abandoned store. Her face brightened with her curious fleeting joy, subdued by ancient pain and disappointment. She whistled to him, her shrill signal also alerting those of the street who had not yet seen him. Parker waved. Her rough voice rattled across the way to him.

"Doc, I need a drink. Can you spring me one?"

He crossed the street to her, his expression concerned. She saw it as no, and her great swollen face lost its small hope. He saw the sudden expression of a hurt child beneath the fat and curdled flesh, then a stony apathy.

"Okay, okay, okay," he said placatingly. "I'll get you something in just a little while."

He looked into the dimness behind her. "Is that the Counselor and Lightning back there? Have they passed out?"

"Yeh," she grunted asthmatically. Her mood took an abrupt turn. She quaked in the chill of new winds which swept off the mountains and flowed down Lexington Street as though it were a funnel or wind chute for the city.

"This is a hell of a place," she suddenly cried and stamped her foot weakly. He stared at her grotesqueness, her unloveliness: the bloated body; the legs, huge and round; the swollen ankles bundled in cheap wrappings of old, tattered cloth; the tiny feet in small, scuffed shoes. Her ulcerous face was as ridged as the mountains surrounding the city. She gestured toward the two prostrate bodies behind her.

"Look at them. They are like my family. I pray for them. I pray for everybody here. I try to look out for them, but I'm puny now. Things are going wrong inside of me. I gave up on myself a long time ago, but I pray for them.

Parker ached, waited in silence, then shrugged.

"Well, tell His Honor there that I would like a word with him when he comes to," he said; then he crossed the street and went into Wally's Grill. Wally adjusted his spectacles, recognized him, and came the length of the bar toward him. Two nondescript customers sat in beery despair in a booth. Wally was awkward with Dr. Parker, uncomfortable in a way that the citizens of skid row were not.

"How you is?" Wally asked in a faint imitation of dialect.

"I is personally okay. How you?" Parker responded.

"It's a bad day. A hard day. I won't take in enough to pay the light bill."

"Coffee, then, and a bowl of chili. How much do you think Big Nell weighs?"

"I can tell you exactly. They had her at the state hospital in Morganton two months ago, and she weighed three hundred and thirty-seven pounds. When she got out, she came straight here to pawn her suitcase. It had the commitment papers inside, along with a pack of Tums and somebody's brassiere that wouldn't even go around her wrist, for God's sake. I read the papers, and that's how I know how much she weighs. I gave the brassiere to a young whore from Henderson County . . ."

His eyes widened comically.

"I got nothing, no, nothing, in return. Anyway, Nell's in bad shape."

"All of them out there are in bad shape," Parker said. "They get to me, or they did. I've tried to stop reacting emotionally, telling myself that I'm only here to do a study in sociology."

"Yeh, the losers here like you. They know you're goodhearted," Wally said.

"People anywhere welcome a scribe who will write down a part of their history. Everyone has a history. The Counselor probably has a wide and varied one. I feel that he could somehow be resurrected."

Wally's smile was knowing. "No," he said, "not that one. The Reverend Tottle has tried for years. The Counselor is like all the others. He got knocked sideways in the road a long time ago, and they pushed him off down here to rust."

"I'm beginning to see it differently," Parker said. "They are mountain people, most of them. They or their immediate ancestors came off the land. Out there they had spirit because they were free, hardy. They came to town and were labeled 'hillbillies' or 'rednecks' and were pushed aside—like the Nazis' herding undesirables into camps, but much more subtly. They brought no wealth to town with them; therefore they attracted no wealth. Towns have social categories, all based on money— upper class, middle, lower-middle, lower period—and on Lexington? Redneck trash. It's a new kind of ethnic slur, Wally.

The word 'nigger' is passé and crude. People who have learned
to wince at 'nigger' toss the word 'redneck' around. Maybe
it's a way to get off the hook with the blacks. God, it is to
laugh."

Wally shook his head. This kind of talk was the very thing
that made him uncomfortable with Parker. Wally suspected
that the professor was trying to push things into his mind, and
his brain didn't like it. He moved away and began to load beer
into the coolers. The two drinkers left. Parker pondered other
things.

The sky grew darker. Now the clouds passed in giant gray
heaps, dingy glaciers moving across the sky. The cold thrusting
corners of old buildings shone moistly in the glimmer of
streetlights now beginning to come on. A billion points of light
splashed and died as cold rain beat on the pavement. The wind
gusted through the streets, roared with a vast, throaty breath,
trailed off to far mountains, then came again, a frozen whip.

The slash of rain lifted the Counselor and Lightning from
their stupor, and Parker saw them swaying and tottering
stiffly around Big Nell in the dim storefront. They came
quickly to Wally's. The Counselor spoke in a voice cracking
and belligerent.

"You got any money, Professor?" he demanded.

Parker stared at the red-eyed hulk of man, grimy and be-
whiskered; then at Lightning, the slight, bent bird's skeleton,
hunched from past vicissitudes and from those yet to come.

"Wine for the Counselor and his companion," Parker said
in feigned cheer. Wally brought a quart and two paper cups.

"Use the cups so the bottle don't chip whatever teeth you
have left," Wally said.

The Counselor scowled. "Impertinent! Your familiarity is
out of place," he said, raising a trembling cup.

"Remember, he's the man which has the wine," Lightning
reminded him.

"Damn, you better lap it out of a saucer. You're gonna shake it all out of that cup," Wally said. The Counselor glared at him.

"I trust you'll save some of that for Big Nell," Parker said.

The Counselor drank deeply and kept the wine down. He belched and drank again, then settled down a bit.

"Now, Professor, I believe you asked to see me?"

Parker laughed. "Yes, I left word with your secretary. I want to talk to you, but if you think I asked to see you—I asked Big Nell to tell you I wanted a word with you—oh God, forget it," he said wearily. "Yes, I asked to see you."

"Well, here I am. Get on with it."

"Can you spare the time from your busy schedule? That is the question."

"You know, I always mean to ask. Just exactly what are you a professor of?" the Counselor asked suspiciously.

"Sociology, though I also have a degree in philosophy."

"Ah, yes, philosophy, a way to see the world. I don't now see it," the Counselor admitted.

"Perhaps you can find a way to resume your life in better circumstances."

"No, he's bound fer hell," Lightning said. "He's a-goin' straight to hell unless Preacher Tottle saves him."

"Hell?" Parker asked. "In one old way of looking at it, hell is merely the draining and fading away of shapes and forms so that energy may be reformed in another shape on a plane not now visible to us. Hell is a dance of energy, slow and fast."

The Counselor's head rolled about unsteadily. "I am ready," he said. "Let the dances of hell begin."

"Begin?" Parker said. "They began a hundred million years ago. I would like a word in private with you, if you don't mind."

The portly man looked at him, bit his lip.

"All right. Lightning, go to the other end of the bar."

They watched Lightning's poky and graceless walk away from them.

"Counselor, you know that I feel you are too much of a

person to waste away here. I want you to consider leaving
Lexington Street and going to a farm in the mountains near
Boone. I admit that it is a strict place, run by religious funda-
mentalists, but they will keep you for three months and dry
you out, and by then we can arrange a program of rehabilita-
tion."

The Counselor shook his head. His face showed that peculiar
hurt-child expression of the wino. He grew deeply defensive.

"I'm doing what I want to do . . . won't go . . . can't leave
. . . don't want to dry out . . ."

Parker buried his face in his hands. "All right. Have some
more wine, but think about it. It's a better place than this."

He stared outside at the gloomy light on the street. The
Counselor's eyes cut about sharply in his puffy flesh.

"What's wrong with it here?" he demanded. "All my friends
are here."

"I said have some more wine, for God's sake," Parker said.

They grew silent. Night fell quickly. Shadows moved in the
alleys. The Counselor and Lightning went out. Occasional,
small neon signs flickered poisonous color in the deepening
night. The tired old buildings, tossed together in accidental
conglomeration years ago, now sagged in great decrepitude,
tilting on warped and rotting foundations. Streets of ancient,
chipped brick pushed upward through a patchwork of asphalt.
The rain sloped earthward, beat and ran and puddled where
the asphalt had been eaten by the weathers.

Parker stared out at the men moving like fish in a murky
stream—broken, shabby men. In pairs, in threes and fours, they
emerged from the deeper shadows to wander aimlessly. They
joined to conspire, to pool their resources. Then one entered a
bar and returned with a bottle. The unholy brotherhood,
founded on lostness and loneliness, faded into the alleys. Parker drank his fourth cup of coffee. Wally stood nearby.

"I'm waiting for the Reverend Tottle," Parker said.

"Hell, stay all night if you have to. This street ain't much of
a place fer a university man."

"Well, it isn't much of a university, either."

"Not, huh?"

"No, it's just like the town. This whole place is snake-bit. A small college pretends it's a university because some pathetic civic leaders want to boast that they have a university here, a Harvard-on-the-hill. Inadequate professors support the fantasy. The others laugh. The students don't know the difference. A small, incredibly provincial, schizophrenic town pretends to be another Charlotte or Atlanta. And people go along with it."

Wally laughed. "It's a crazy place. One time I heard my doctor laughing on the phone with another doctor. He said the town first went crazy in a big land boom in the twenties and bankrupted itself. The government let them set up a sinking fund to pay off the debt. That took forty years. They got it paid down to almost nothing when these idiotic big wheels went wild again—ambition is worse than likker and women—and built a civic center that nobody much uses but everybody has to pay for. That's where my taxes go. To pay fer big-shot ideas. They don't worry about it. But if you criticize them, you know what they say?"

"What?"

"Love it or leave it."

"How about love it or shove it?"

Wally laughed.

"That's why this town is so mediocre. The bright people accepted the invitation," Parker said.

"Yeh, they do say the smart ones around here go someplace else," Wally said.

"Well, they're still gone," Parker said. "The pissants have inherited the earth. The losers won."

"I don't really understand why you come here and watch these people and write in your notebook."

Parker shrugged. "A study is a study. For various professional reasons, some professors conduct their obscure studies around here. Some of them do it with wild hopes for textbook

publication. Some do it for reasons known to no man, not even
to themselves. It is a part of the act of being a professor. It is
better than sinking in puerile college politics. Lexington Street
is one of the exciting, challenging places in this town if you
look at it the right way."

The door opened and the Reverend Tottle came in, distrustful of the place, disapproving of it, but himself an indisputable
part of the street. His tight lips had a barely charitable, yet
groveling smile. Thin spectacles rode on a long ridge of nose,
and a dark suit hung shapeless on his diminished rib cage. He
appeared more malnourished than some of the winos. At one
time in his life, Tottle had felt in his heart an ache for humanity
and a pain for the miserable condition of man. He had taken
this sentiment to be a religious call, a summons to minister.
Without benefit of higher education, seminary, or denomina-
tional ties, he took up the Bible and the cross and came to the
gray vacancy of Lexington Street to fish for men. His place,
The New Hope Mission of the Voice of Elijah Tabernacle
("Rev. Austin Tottle, ordained by the Holy Ghost" was written in uncertain handscript beneath the larger printing) was
financed by various sects which donated small sums to the
project. The mission was open three nights a week for preaching and stew.

"Professor?" Tottle said, advancing timidly.

"How are you, Reverend?" Parker asked.

"Fine, fine. The Lord bless you, brother, and I need a favor.
It is something in the name of Jesus. I am in need and I am told
to ask and I shall receive."

"How much do you want?"

"Ah, well, it is not money that I seek, although I will say
that money is always needed for the work of the Lord."

"What, then?"

"Do you know that brother McKinley Moore died in jail
today?"

"Oh no? The one-legged beggar? Died? What happened?"

"His time was up. Overdue, to be frank. The Lord took him

on to a better place. The beer-joint owners on Lexington took up a small collection for me to preach a service for him in the mission tomorrow night. The county will bury him the next day."

"Good! What can I do?"

"Well, I don't know what to say. I'm sorry to admit it but he was a mean and vile old man who cussed a lot and I just know he's gone to hell. I can't think of anything to say."

"Well, be true to yourself and don't preach then."

"The owners of these joints want it. I'm afraid if I don't, they'll quit donating to the mission. I'll be able to preach, but I need you to write the words for me. If you'll do that—a few words—then I'll preach. The Lord will somehow put the words in my mouth."

Parker leaned back. The big pane in Wally's window bent in the wind, and waves of rain smeared the length of it. He suddenly realized how much comfort there was for the homeless in these low taverns. Haven, warmth, a place of some small cheer. Hold back the night. Stay the rain, the wind. A sermon? Why not?

"Of course I will. When do you need it?"

"By tomorrow night. I thank you. Truly Professor, I thank you. The Lord forbade my mind, but for the sake of the mission I do believe I'll feel right in reading it."

Tottle went into the night. Parker stared at the steam condensing at the edge of the window. He took out his pad and scribbled a few notes. Wally offered to refill his coffee cup.

"No, I have an early class and I need to write something," he said. He buttoned up his coat, pulled his rain hat low, and walked several blocks to his car in the old, dead city.

In an alley, the Counselor and Lightning huddled. They were barely visible to each other in a feeble gray shaft of light which filtered down from a dirty window high on the side of a building. The Counselor held up a bottle and shook it. Royal grape, almost gone. Lightning's lizard face was pinched and morose.

"Look in yer pocket again, man," he pleaded in a reedy whine. Somewhere in his fog of memory, the little man was aware that his companion had some coins. He also knew that the Counselor would hide soup from his starving mother.

"It is no use, my friend," snapped the bigger man impatiently. "Surely you do not believe that I would hold out on you? My good man, my good fellow, my gooo . . . ooo . . . ooddd friend," and his heavy face showed hurt, wounded honor. His mind floated past the image of a quarter and a dime in his shoe. He wiggled the bottle again.

"Nell said McKinley died today," he said abruptly.

"McKinley Moore? Where?"

"City jail. Dead and in hell."

Then he tilted the bottle and drank. He wiped his whiskers and handed over the bottle.

"By God," Lightning said. "You got me to feeling sorry for McKinley, then you killed the wine."

"No, no, no, my good man. There's yet a dram there."

"There ain't enough to help," Lightning said. Nevertheless, he drank.

They stood silent and pensive and trembled as the quickening wind brought a deeper chill into the damp alley. The alcohol flared briefly in them, warmed them. Runnels of water snaked swiftly through the alley floor and passed through the broken leather of their shoes. Lightning shifted his weight, and the water squished between his toes. He slowly gazed downward, his eyes like those of a dazed salamander.

"We can't stay here tonight. Let's go back to where Nell is."

"I don't think that's a good idea," the Counselor said impatiently. "I told her two things. I told her we would bring her a drink, and I told her we would help her get in the back of that broken-down old Ford behind Wally's place. She needs to stretch out awhile. We're able neither to move her nor to take her a drink."

"That's right," Lightning said. "I'm as weak as cat piss.

I've just got three pennies. If we had twenty-eight more, we could get a small lasher of port apiece."

"Yes, of course. More. God yes," the Counselor said.

He turned away in the darkness and shuddered at the wreckage of his life, the ruin. He blurted:

"Holy God! How did I sink to this ocean floor of scum?"

He tilted his head sideways to the leaking sky as if to question an entity who had set him down here to learn some obscure lesson. Flashes of intelligence and education were still to be found under the webbing of dissipation. Self-pity and frustration had printed other hieroglyphs on his face. The hoary pelt of his hair lifted in the wind, and his frame trembled.

In another time, another town, he had been renowned for wit, a piercing rapier of a mind. Once there had been home and family, an industrious life. After a hard day in the courtroom, home, and dinner, there was the friendly decanter and a drink for the weariness and for the pride—which everyone calls ego and which is not ego, but pride—skidding, wounding, hurtful pride. At the end of each day, each crisis, there was a drink, and the drink itself became a crisis. Life grew to be a mocking and empty task. A drink.

In those blind days, everything rotted out from under him. Occasionally he rallied long enough to wonder if he could call back those easy surrenders and unravel the long skeins of calamity. In rare moments, he promised himself that one day he would leave Lexington Street and rise to new heights—resolutions of no substance, half-thoughts that lingered like a cloud-veiled moon in an infant's dream. Here he had standing among the zombies of this forgotten street. He had status in this low cabal. Anonymity, grayness in a surge of hopelessness. His fellow ciphers were impressed by the eloquence of the Counselor. They needed his rhetoric, his drunken outrage, the bilious tirades which gave voice, expression, genius to each man's defeat and living death. For them all he cursed the fiendishness of a society which had no place for him and—as he generously expressed it to those fawning about him—his colleagues. It comforted them to count among their number a man of his background. The tides had washed ashore strange baggage here among the prowling bands of drunks, cheap hookers, panhandlers, petty thieves. There was not a reliable informer or a full criminal among them, detectives said. Nevertheless, they had long ago accepted the Counselor, and he, them; now they owned each other.

In the dim light, Lightning stared at the shaggy, drooping countenance of the Counselor with some envy. He often resented the proud, patronizing air of the larger man. But inside the clogged gray circuits of Lightning's brain burned faint curiosity about the Counselor's strange ways. The Counselor played roles far beyond the ken of his small companion. He could drop his grandiose manner and mooch money from passers-by in abject tones of humility, tell tales of misfortune which, coupled with his manner, were too fantastic to disbelieve. Many coins came his way. Lightning could show no background, no history. He was a zero, neither adding to nor taking away from the drab hue of the street.

The Counselor rumbled again. He pulled his frayed, wet collar closer to his neck and then stared up into the circling rain, which turned to sleet even as he watched.

"We can't sleep here," he said, his hoarse voice cracking. "I truly curse the dreadful, goddamned day I came here to his hive of cold, uncaring, uncharitable demons. The day was cursed when I first put glass to lip. God damn it, I say, God damn it all. Where did it begin? Where will it end?"

He subsided. The ice came in swirling torrents as they stepped from the alley into the hushed, brooding street. Now and then other travelers of the night shuffled across the street, disappearing into another alley.

They went to the storefront. The dim glow from a light down the street faintly limned Big Nell, outlined her as the bulky, shapeless guardian of a deep, black grotto. She was crying softly.

"Did you get something?" she asked.

"No, no," the Counselor said.

"Don't lie to me, you big-shot sonofabitch. I can smell it from here. Did you bring me any?"

"No, we drank it all. It wasn't much and it wasn't good. Why are you crying?"

"If you had any a-tall on a night like this, it was good. I dozed off and dreamed about my little girl."

"Girl? You had a daughter?"

"Yes, yes, I dreamed of her. She was so young and pretty. I dreamed she was dead and many people came to the funeral. She was happy and I was happy and for some reason everyone was happy and I heard someone say that he was so glad she was dead because she would go to a place so pretty."

She began weeping and stuttering and cursing in a barely audible tone; her profanity showed the deterioration of her mind even as the broken veins and piled capillaries and cells showed the deterioration of her body. The Counselor looked about nervously.

"Where is she now, Nell?" he asked, strangely gentle, sober.

"Dead. She is dead," Nell said. "The dream is a sign. McKinley being dead is a sign too. It's a bad sign."

"Sign, hell. It doesn't signal anything to come. The worst has already come for McKinley."

"I dunno," she said. "He told me not long ago that he'd outlive me. He was gifted in those ways."

The Counselor left the storefront and went through the weather to the old Ford, where he knew there were two old coats, and brought them back. Then they helped Nell off her crate and stumbled to the back of their cavern, where they sat huddled under the coats. They fell asleep, moaning and jerking with their dreams. As they slept, snow began blowing through the streets, and by dawn there was a two-inch carpet on the pavement, and still it came down.

Classes at the college closed because of the snow. Parker

went to the police station, and the jailer showed him the cell where McKinley had died, then directed him to the records section. Parker checked McKinley's record, then went to Wally's Grill and drafted a short sermon for the Reverend Tottle.

The Counselor came in and drew Wally into a whispered, excited conversation. Wally nodded, his face concerned. Then he said to Parker, "Hey, how about keeping an eye on things for a minute. I need to go see about Nell."

"Sure. What's wrong?"

"He says she is doing porely. I'll go see."

Parker watched them through the window as they crossed to Nell's grotto. He saw her wide, full face swing around, the brows visible, the eyes wide and dumb. When they returned, Wally bustled about, then handed the Counselor three hot dogs, three cups of coffee, and two pints of wine.

"Thanky, indeed thanky," the Counselor said. "We'll pay you sometime, brother. Your reward will come."

Through the window Wally and Parker watched them eating and drinking. The Counselor's feet were moving in a brisk little jig step. Wally shook his head.

"Damn," he said.

"I'll be back about seven," Parker said, arising. "Are you going to Tottle's mission tonight?"

"No. Why in hell would I go there? I never do."

"They're going to have a service for McKinley. The county is paying for a funeral. They're going to have a service for him tonight and bury him in the morning if they can get the ground open."

"Oh yeh, I forgot. McKinley."

The Counselor and Lightning left Nell with a pint and moved out onto other streets to begin begging. The air was bitterly cold and the streets slick with ice. They made no significant scores, picking up only a few coins at the bus stops.

They were asked to leave several business places. Darkness, cold and foreboding, came as they turned again into Lexington Street. They had gone only a few steps when the swelling dirge from the mission's organ overrode the wail of the wind. The Counselor stopped, his mood rising. He cocked an ear in exaggerated attention.

"By God, by God, the mission. It had escaped my mind that tonight was the night. Ah, the good, good Reverend Tottle. Excellent cuisine," he murmured, stroking his stubble with a splayed finger. "Ah yes, come, my good and trusted friend, let us now go into the House of the Lord. Stew, fit only for gourmands such as we. Too, let us not overlook the possibility that we might be saved—aye, washed through the veritable blood, saved, and then beat this unholy, confounded, and hellish street. May we yet recover our faith?"

Lightning jerked spastically in the wind and rubbed his thin nose. "I ain't never had any faith to begin with. You make me nervous talking like that. Ye have to be careful in there. They'll run ye crazy."

"Come. The sermon will be good for the recovery of our souls, and the stew will keep our bodies together. On these two points hang all the law and the profits, haw, haw . . ." he boomed. One veined eyelid dropped in a solemn wink, and a grimy finger pointed into the air.

"I am the alpha and the amigo," he intoned and looked slyly at Lightning. The joke was lost on his companion. The wind took his wit.

"Ah well, come now, let us be off to the warmth and hospitality of our Christian brother's inn. For sure, it does him a world of good to help us. Never get in the way of a Christian who's trying to help you."

The signboard overhead creaked in the wind as they drew close. The tantalizing odor of beef stew breathed from the door, and the organ moaned in ponderous descriptions of glory. When the music stopped, they stepped inside. They saw the casket, and the Counselor retched, blanched, and reached weakly for a seat. Lightning swayed in shock.

"What in the goddamned hell?" the Counselor gasped. Fellow derelicts reached out to help them.

"It's jis' ol' McKinley, that's all," one of them said. "He died yesterday. Tottle is going to try to preach him into heaven from here."

"McKinley, eh? Well, well," the Counselor said, settling down. "Well done, old friend. Good and faithful servant. It's been a long time since I went to a friend's funeral. Ah, the beauty of the ritual. The pity, the pity."

The minutes dragged. Tottle alternately paced the floor and played more music on the organ. Two women—do-gooders from some congregation—were with him. One was fat, warted, righteous. The other was skinny, bespectacled. She kept her eyes away from the casket. Suddenly Wally walked through the door and up the short aisle.

"Have you seen brother Parker?" Tottle asked.

"No, but he told me he was coming."

"Maybe it's the weather," the preacher said.

In fact, Parker's car had frozen, and he was delayed. As soon as he could get there, he parked at the bottom of Lexington Street and walked up the hill. He glanced toward Wally's closed joint, then saw Nell in the back of her grotto. Suddenly he wheeled and went to her. She had been dead long enough to be stiff. He shone a penlight into her face and saw that a tear had frozen in her eye—a small, perfect, pear-shaped crystal. It picked up the beam from his flashlight and flashed back a blue glint, with whorls of red and gold like a fine diamond. He stood there a few moments, bearing the burden of death on a bad night. Then he made his way slowly over the ice to the mission. He banged through the door and into the warm stew-smell and the sight of the cheap casket. The motley congregation turned. The Reverend Tottle smiled. Wally was slumped in the back row. The preacher came to meet him.

"You have it? You have a sermon, a few words?"

Parker fixed his eyes on the preacher with difficulty.

"Yes, yes," he said, "here it is."

Tottle looked at the page a moment, then gave it back to Parker.

"Ah, Professor," he said gingerly, "I wonder . . . I say, I don't think I can do it. Perhaps the Lord has forbidden me, after all. Yet right back there sits one of the businessmen. It must be done. Can you do it for me? Will you please read it for us?"

Parker smiled grimly and nodded. The women stared at him in awkward anticipation. Tottle held up a small brass bell in one thin hand. He gave it an experimental wiggle, then rang loudly. Everyone faced forward obediently.

"Brothers, our good friend McKinley lays here a corpse. The Lord has asked, and so Professor Parker has agreed to say a few words. When he has done with it, I'll say a few words in behalf of the Lord."

Parker went to the pulpit. "What the hell?" he muttered. He looked at the scattered few, who were mostly sober, somehow expectant. They awaited his words. Someone must speak for McKinley. Then he felt a surge and knew that, for the time, he was truly one of them. He smiled and spoke.

"Well, unaccustomed as I am, as we say. Now, McKinley Moore was a man with whom we were all familiar. I am not remiss in saying that we loved him in our fashion. If he had a home, it was the city jail. So may we not correctly state that McKinley died in peace at his home, despite the efforts of various do-gooders like myself to urge him from time to time to find a better home."

They were sitting upright. He paused.

"McKinley also went regularly to his winter home at Craggy, which you all know is the prison camp down by the river. Now we must ask, since prison implies offenses against society, what was McKinley's main offense against the society in which he lived?"

They waited.

"McKinley got drunk, often and well. If we may look at drunkenness as a man's life work, something of accomplishment, then McKinley raised it to a high art. He got spectacularly drunk at any given opportunity. A heinous thing, to get drunk. For that offense he paid. McKinley Moore built a life sentence in prison. I have seen his record—fourteen single-spaced pages—for being drunk on Lexington Street. He served a life sentence thirty days at a time.

"So here we are, to send this broken-down, one-legged old man with gray whiskers down the river one last time. He will go, or has gone, to a new place. I suspect it to be a place the reverse of this one. There the judged will be the judges. Their sentences may not be quite so harsh as those leveled on this side, because they will know what they are doing. McKinley Moore now knows, I presume, about mercy and/or the lack of it. He will also know, by now, of justice which is not an abstract theory to be taken lightly. Justice will be done, do not doubt it.

"If you here worry that real justice will fail to come about, do not worry. It is working even now. The things you are guilty of are small things, nothings, compared to the immense evils in the hearts of other men.

"This is all I want to say about McKinley. The preacher here says he has a few words, and after he finishes, I want to tell you one thing more," Parker said.

Tottle arose and motioned to someone in the kitchen. A young man in a blue suit and heavy coat came to wheel the casket up the aisle and out the door, where the hearse waited to return the body to the funeral home. Parker sat down beside the women. The preacher leaned over him and whispered confidentially:

"It is too much, sometimes. It is just too much. I was called to do the Lord's work, but it is a hardship on me. These people are trash. It burns me up. They could work somewhere if they would. I believe I've outgrown this ministry. I appreciate what you've done. Now I'm going to put the gospel on them before I feed them."

Tottle advanced to the pulpit, his nervousness falling away. He faced them, the furtive men, the listless men, the hungry men, guilty of defeat. The drab men.

He began softly as they knew he would and talked about pleasant things, the good, holy, and righteous life. The sinners began to relax. The two women kept their eyes primly to the front. Three times a week he started out on the side of the lost. Then he grew louder, as they knew he would. They braced. He became personal. They hid behind stone faces. "He is the man which has the stew," Lightning was fond of saying. He laid on fury, thunder, fire, brimstone, threats, dismal promises. Parker sat in wretched embarrassment.

Tottle softened his voice, switched styles. In a low voice he entreated them. Here and there in the congregation a sniffle sounded as a heart was touched by its own plight. Tottle sensed a rewarding night.

The Counselor leaned forward, sobered, following closely. A forgotten sense of courtroom drama stirred in his brain. Somewhere, under earthen tons of despair, the Counselor's buried hope struggled. Parker caught it immediately. He too leaned forward.

The pulse at the Counselor's temple was visible. He stared at Tottle, at a land beyond him. Tottle felt it: a drowning soul had signaled for the lifeline. He was astounded. Something transcendent was going on out there. He redoubled his effort. He preached to the point of rant—he implored and he commanded, he beseeched and he prayed. The Counselor sat on the edge of his seat. Sweat beaded his craggy face. His lumpy jaws clenched and clamped, and the thick hawser of his neck knotted with bulging veins. He sought to extricate the keys to the kingdom from the howled sermon. Then he slumped back.

Tottle stopped abruptly. The tautness was gone. He did not

know what had happened. Had he actually converted one? Briefly, absently, he asked for decision. They all stood to be saved once again. Tottle entered their number in a notebook under the heading, "The Saved," and gave a closing benediction. Parker watched the Counselor go straight for Tottle.

"Yes sir, brother, I've been saved," the Counselor said. "The ring of fire fell about me and burned away my worst desires and cravings. I can tell it. I'm turning away henceforth. A ghastly end awaits, as you said. Well put, sir, well put. Those things you say are right. Everybody in the Jesus business knows it to be true. Uh, I didn't mean for it to sound quite so, well, like that. All we have to do is straighten up and mend our ways, right. There's no possibility that you are wrong. I admit that."

The wind screamed and the door clattered. Parker's voice shot across the room like a shellburst.

"Preacher, are you going to let these men sleep here tonight?"

Tottle flushed. The women stared at the floor.

"Well, ah yes, of course. I can consider that. Of course they can pile up right here in the floor. It is not a bedding mission but they can certainly sleep right here on this cold floor."

"It's not half as cold here as it is out there. I want to tell you something, gentlemen—and ladies. As I came up here I found Big Nell frozen to death on her crate. I mean she is dead."

A strange vitality came over their faces. Their wretched brows twisted in disbelief. Parker walked slowly down the aisle, and they fell in line behind him. They tramped in a column down the street, their broken shoes crunching in the snow and ice as they went. They ran the last few steps and crowded around Nell's grotto, squinting, trying to see her in the gloom. Wally brought a flashlight and shone it on her.

"Damn," one said. "She froze to death right here. At least ol' McKinley got in the jail. They quit putting her up. They didn't want her there. You're in bad shape when they won't let you in the jail."

"Do you know why they wouldn't take her in jail?" Parker asked.

"She beshit herself all the time. She didn't have no control. Besides, they was afraid she'd die in jail and they'd get blamed fer it in the newspapers."

Wally stepped forward and touched her. "She's like cold marble," he said.

They moved toward her in the cold, cavernous storefront, a dark, gathered force of lost anger. The flashlight shone on the frozen tear at the edge of Nell's eye, and the ice glinted. The moment became a rare tribal occasion when the queen's time is at an end and she is leaving, but as she sits, enthroned in her royal cave for the last time, they witness the formation and brief life of a precious jewel, her last jewel. They could not cry. Their feelings were shattered like bottles in the city dump, scattered and buried too deep. She had cried for them all.

They stared at the last tear. It sparkled for a bright, peaceful, moment like a star in a winter sky. Wally reached cautiously to touch it. The tear fell and disappeared into Nell's bunched collar. Wally looked at Parker. His breath was a long, gray rope.

"I didn't know tears froze, did you?"

"I never would have thought about it. Did you think they didn't?"

Wally shrugged. "I never thought about it either."

The Counselor pushed Lightning forward. "Look at her, by God," he said. "She was our friend. We slept with her last night. She shivered and shook and moaned and took on all night. She said yesterday that she had dreamed her daughter was dead. I wonder if her daughter *is* dead?"

Wally clamped his chattering teeth and shook his head.

"She ain't got no daughter," he said.

Suddenly they were bathed in a brilliant spotlight. They all turned quickly to see a police van on the street behind them.

"What is it now?" a cop asked.

"Nothin' much," one of them said wearily, cynically. "Somebody is dead is all."

"All right, nobody move. Hands up. Who done it?"

One of the derelicts giggled weakly.

"Hit's jis' a ol' dead woman. Big Nell is dead, that's all."

Two officers were among them, their pistols raised. One reached and touched her, and she toppled sideways.

"Hey man. Goddamn," someone complained. "That ol' woman ain't a-botherin' you now."

The officer caught Nell, pushed her back into place.

"Sorry," he said politely. "Hell, I'm sorry. Hey, get on the radio and tell them to get a meat wagon down here, or an ambulance or whatever you call it without hurting anybody's feelings. Shit! Drunks."

Two more cruisers pulled up and four officers got out. A young one began shouting.

"What the hell is going on? What're you damn losers milling around here for?" he barked.

They stirred and muttered. The young cop fingered his pistol butt. Ruby blades of red light whirled across the snow as an ambulance approached.

"Looky there," Lightning said, nudging Parker. The preacher was locking the door to the mission.

"He went back on his word. Now we ain't got no place," Lightning said. He began sobbing and snuffling. The Counselor was growing bellicose. The group was milling and the cops were growing nervous. Wally stood a little apart so that he wouldn't be too closely identified with the derelicts, yet he chattered on with them in sympathy. One of the policemen went to him.

"You trying to start trouble, Wally?" he demanded.

"No, I don't want no trouble. I just don't see why you can't put 'em all in jail where it's warm."

"Because the goddamned sheriff is afraid they'll die up there and he'll get blamed for it. He gave us a list of all the old drunks we can't lock up anymore, and Nell headed the list."

Parker watched in rising fury as the preacher, after locking the mission, headed for his car with the women. He ran up the street, catching them just as the preacher was unlocking his car.

"Preacher, you said the men could stay there tonight."

"Well, I've changed my mind. They can't stay. The fire code . . . my license to preach . . . oh God, I'm stopping this. I'm sick of it. I can't stand it anymore. I'm through, through, through."

A strange light came in Parker's eyes.

"Reverend Tottle, I want you to come over here where the police are for a moment. You can be a big help. Please." He pulled the preacher from the car.

"He'll be back soon," Parker said to the ladies, an insane leer on his face. He pulled Tottle down the street. They found Wally and the Counselor, both standing apart from the muttering derelicts and cursing the police. Then the Counselor crossed the street to rail against the situation.

"Nobody moves until the captain gets here," one of the officers said, beating his palm with his billy. The wind rose and everyone instinctively packed closer together.

"I want to get out of here," Tottle said, sniffing.

"What did you say?" an officer asked from the center of the clot of men in the doorway.

"I'm a minister . . ." said Tottle.

"A do-gooder, huh? You'll do good to shut up. This might be murder," the officer said.

"You better believe it," Parker said.

"What?" the officer shouted belligerently. Parker dragged Tottle closer. Parker reached past one of the winos to an officer's belt and snatched his billy club.

"Here!" he said and handed it to Tottle, who was nonplussed.

"You have to quit playing God," the preacher whimpered.

"I'm not playing. I'm perfectly serious," Parker said.

"All right, enough is enough," the officer said and pushed toward them.

"To hell with you, pig. I'll beat your head in," Parker hissed under his breath and pushed Tottle forward. The cop hit Tottle in the jaw, and he fell on the street. The club clattered on the ice and bounced almost to Wally across the street. Parker laughed happily. The officer spun him about and hit him in the mouth with his fist.

"You bleeding liberal sonofabitch," he said.

Parker went down, then rose to his knees, fumbling with his teeth.

"Jesus," he said. "My crowns. You broke my crowns."

The officer stood over him, raging.

"Crowns? I'll break your neck . . ."

Another police car skidded to a stop on the ice, its blue light flashing.

"Well, here's High Pockets and Pip; let them decide," an officer said. Immediately the tall shift captain and his lieutenant were out, pushing the derelicts into a manageable bunch. Nobody moved. Tottle moaned and raised his head. The tall captain looked around sternly, feeling the bitter wind rising.

"Put 'em all in jail but Wally, by God," he said.

"They're on that list, Captain," an officer said.

"Well, don't charge 'em with being drunk. They ain't drunk. I want 'em charged with assaulting officers, impeding investigations, resisting arrest, obstructing justice—any damn thing. Charge 'em with anything."

"Will it hold up in court?" the officer asked dubiously.

The captain stared at him. "It'll hold up through the night," he said. "Who are them two on the deck? Get 'em up and jail 'em. Throw 'em in the paddywagon with these winos. Give 'em a good ride to the jail."

As Parker got into the van, he looked at Wally in the strange light bouncing off the snow from the street light, grinned, and held up his hand.

Then, with great courtesy, the policemen stood outside their cars and waited for the ambulance attendants to load Big Nell. They brought her slowly out of the doorway to the ambulance. Wally looked at the captain, who stood in stiff, military respect as the doors closed on her. The ambulance pulled away, followed by the police car and van.

Wally stared across the empty street to where Nell's crate lay beside an old coat. Nothing moved on Lexington except a few creaking old signs blown by the wind and the snow that fluttered past the street lights.